"How about the boys ranch for Corey?" Darcy asked.

"I know they have room for one more boy," Nick said, "and I'd much rather see Corey there, but I'm not sure it'll happen. I volunteer at the boys ranch, and it would be great for Corey."

Darcy wasn't surprised that Nick would volunteer there. In the short time she'd been with him, she saw a man of action and heart. "Then I'll pray that something is done for Corey."

Nick looked away. "In my experience He hasn't helped much."

There was something in Nick's voice that touched Darcy. Who did he turn to when he was in trouble or upset?

She started to say something, but the tense set of his jaw and rigid posture indicated this wasn't a good time. He wouldn't hear her.

She didn't want to leave Haven until something was done for Corey. How could she walk away from a child in need?

And how could she walk away from Nick McGarrett?

* * *

Lone Star Cowboy League: Boys Ranch
Bighearted ranchers in small-town Texas

The Rancher's Texas Match by Brenda Minton
October 2016

The Ranger's Texas Proposal by Jessica Keller
November 2016

The Nanny's Texas Christmas by Lee Tobin McClain
December 2016

The Cowboy's Texas Family by Margaret Daley
January 2017

The Doctor's Texas Baby by Deb Kastner
February 2017

The Rancher's Texas Twins by Allie Pleiter
March 2017

Margaret Daley, an award-winning author of ninety books (five million sold worldwide), has been married for over forty years and is a firm believer in romance and love. When she isn't traveling, she's writing love stories, often with a suspense thread, and corralling her three cats, who think they rule her household. To find out more about Margaret, visit her website at margaretdaley.com.

Books by Margaret Daley

Love Inspired

Lone Star Cowboy League: Boys Ranch

The Cowboy's Texas Family

Lone Star Cowboy League

A Baby for the Rancher

Caring Canines

Healing Hearts
Her Holiday Hero
Her Hometown Hero
The Nanny's New Family

A Town Called Hope

His Holiday Family
A Love Rekindled
A Mom's New Start

The Firefighter Daddy

Visit the Author Profile page at Harlequin.com for more titles.

The Cowboy's Texas Family

Margaret Daley

Special thanks and acknowledgment
are given to Margaret Daley for her contribution to the
Lone Star Cowboy League: Boys Ranch miniseries.

Recycling programs
for this product may
not exist in your area.

ISBN-13: 978-0-373-89902-9

The Cowboy's Texas Family

This edition published by arrangement with Love Inspired Books.

www.Harlequin.com

Printed in U.S.A.

Chapter One

Nick McGarrett marched into Fletcher Snowden Phillips's law office in Haven, Texas. It was time the man stepped up and helped a member of his family. Fletcher's secretary looked up and frowned. As Nick crossed to her desk, he glanced at his mud-splattered jeans and boots. When he'd received a tearful call from Corey Phillips, a ten-year-old second cousin of Fletcher's, Nick had come straight from replacing a section of a fence on his ranch.

Nick owed Corey's older brother, Doug. When they'd gone on their last mission together, Nick had promised his combat buddy that after he left the service he would watch out for Corey until Doug could. At the time Nick had thought it would be only a few months until Doug returned home. His friend was killed in that mission by a sniper. Young Corey looked like Doug, who'd always had Nick's back when they had gone on assignments together.

Nick fixed his gaze on Nancy Collins, hoping it would convey his determination. "I need to see Fletcher *now*." He'd lost all patience with the man.

Both of the secretary's eyebrows rose, and her chin came up a notch. "Do you have an appointment?"

He peered at the closed door to Fletcher's inner office—shut tightly like the lawyer's heart. Although she probably knew the answer, Nick said, "No."

"I can schedule one for next week. He's leaving soon."

"That's okay." Nick tipped the brim of his brown Stetson and then pivoted and strode into the corridor.

He planted himself against the wall, reclining back with his arms crossed. He was going to talk to the man one way or another. It was in times like this that Nick wished he had enough money to help Fletcher's cousin financially. All he could do was be there for the ten-year-old who lived twenty miles away in a small town on the other side of Waco.

Today Corey had thought his dad was dead. Nick tried to go over to the small, dilapidated house whenever the boy called. If he couldn't,

Nick would call Mrs. Scott, who lived next door, to help. Today he'd been worried he wouldn't make it in time if something worse had happened to Ned Phillips than drinking too much alcohol. Thankfully the older woman had stayed with Corey, assuring the child that his father would wake up, which he finally did. Truth be told, Corey shouldn't even be living with his alcoholic father, who left the child practically to raise himself. Nick had been there as a kid and knew how hard that was.

The door to the office opened, and Fletcher came out.

Nick pushed himself off the wall and stepped in the man's path. "We need to talk."

"I don't have time."

Fletcher, tall with an imposing paunch, tried to skirt around Nick. He didn't weigh as much as the lawyer, but his body was muscular from hard work. Fletcher's idea of exercise was walking to and from his luxury car. Nick blocked his path. "Make time."

Fletcher scowled. "Is this about Corey again?"

"Yes. You're his closest relative. If you don't want to take the boy and raise him, then at least help Ned buy food and clothing." Nick nearly choked on the first part of the sentence. Fletcher wasn't good father material either.

"I'm not giving Ned a cent. All he would do

is buy more liquor. I'm a bachelor. I always have been. I wouldn't know the first thing about raising a child. Check with Family and Protective Services. That's their job." Fletcher quickly sidestepped and charged down the hall, leaving Nick fuming.

As if he hadn't tried contacting the authorities. The underfunded and overworked Family and Protective Services had more urgent cases to deal with.

Nick took several deep, calming breaths and then followed Fletcher outside to the parking lot. The wind held a fierce chill even for early January. As the lawyer drove away, Nick hurried his pace and welcomed what warmth still lingered in the cab of his old truck.

When Nick had first returned to Haven after being in the army, serving overseas in a war zone, Fletcher had said the same thing—that it was the county's problem, not Fletcher's.

Painful memories from the war zone inundated Nick. It had been over a year since he'd returned home to Haven. Too many comrades had died. He didn't understand why there was so much death and hatred. At first he had prayed, but when he lost one friend while Nick was trying to save his life, he'd stopped talking to God. The Lord obviously wasn't listening.

As Nick left Main Street and the small downtown area, he passed Fletcher parking his car in front of his large antebellum home a few miles outside of Haven. The large three-story house overshadowed everyone else's place nearby. Although he came from a family with a long ranching history, Fletcher didn't live on more than two acres of land. According to Fletcher, ranching was manual labor and beneath him.

The sun near the western horizon sent up streaks of yellow, orange and rose through the darkening blue sky. Even though sunset was less than a half hour away, Nick wore his sunglasses to keep the glare from impeding his driving. Through the last burst of brightness, he glimpsed a car coming toward him. The driver maneuvered it to the shoulder of the two-lane highway and then came to a stop.

As Nick approached, he eased up on the gas. The other car's emergency lights began flashing. A blond-haired woman opened the car door, swung her long legs around and stood. Standing partially on the road in four-inch heels, she glanced at him as he passed her. He made a U-turn and parked not a yard behind her. The chilly wind blew even stronger than before. The moisture-laden air would produce snow later tonight.

Nick climbed from his truck and strolled toward the lady using her expensive sports car as a shield from the cold northern blast.

"Not for two hours? It's getting dark." Her throaty voice with a Southern drawl rose in panic. "I'm in the middle of nowhere." She paused while the person on the other end said something and then she sighed heavily. "Fine. Seven thirty or eight." She disconnected and jammed her phone into her leather coat's pocket.

Her gaze clashed with his, and she backed up against her car door. "I know how to defend myself, mister."

"Against what? The cold? That short leather jacket won't keep you warm." His look skimmed her length, taking in her bare legs and the skirt that came to her knees. She had to be passing through. She had *city gal* stamped all over and, by the looks of her Corvette, was rich too. It wasn't that he thought anyone would harm her, but he couldn't leave her stranded for two hours waiting for a ride from whomever she was talking to.

"When I left Mobile this morning, it was a balmy sixty-five degrees and climbing to eighty until I began heading north in Houston."

"A cold front is pushing through. If you don't want to wait, I can drive you to Haven, the nearest town. I know Slim, who owns the garage. Or if you ran out of gas, I can bring you back some. You're only five miles from Haven."

She straightened. "I didn't run out of gas. I have over half a tank. My check-engine light came on when I left Interstate 45. I was praying I could make it to Haven without a problem."

"Haven?" Why? Who was she visiting? She'd fit in about as well as a fox in a hen house.

"I like a small town. Waco is too big."

"And you're from Mobile?" The last time he checked, Mobile was classified as a city.

"South at Gulf Shores. The pace is a little quieter. I noticed you were heading out of town. I'd hate to take you out of your way." The woman hugged her arms close to her body while she pretended she wasn't freezing.

"I don't live too far from here. A few extra miles won't make any difference." His horses could wait, and after he dropped her off, he'd call Corey and decide if he needed to see him in person tonight or if he could wait until tomorrow.

"I hate to be a bother."

In a short time darkness had totally blanketed the landscape, the only illumination coming from his headlights. He didn't want to leave her alone on the road. There was little crime in the area, but if something happened to her, he'd have a hard time forgiving himself. "It's up to you. But after sundown, it's going to get a lot colder fast." He held out his hand. "By the way, I'm Nick McGarrett."

The woman shook it. "I'm Darcy Hill. And if you're sure you have the time to go back into town, then I'd appreciate a ride to the garage. I have a reservation at the Blue Bonnet Inn."

Reservations? The inn was more of a bed-and-breakfast and did a brisk business in the spring, summer and fall. It was well-known in the state for its hospitality and luxurious accommodations, but in the winter it might be half full at its best. "It's not far from Slim's, right off the main street. You might want to get your luggage. Slim will have to tow your car to Haven, and since it's close to quitting time, he probably won't take a look under the hood till morning."

"After being on the road eleven hours, all I want to do is eat and sleep. I can call my auto service back and cancel if you're sure."

"Yes, ma'am. I'll put your luggage in the back of my truck."

She withdrew her key fob from her pocket and clicked it. The trunk popped open. "I also have some pieces in the passenger seat."

Nick stared at the back area of her sports car, every inch crammed with her belongings. While he emptied the trunk—two suitcases and some soft bags—Darcy took out a couple more pieces from the front seat. "How long are you staying?"

"Not sure yet. For a while."

Nick carried the luggage to his truck. *Who makes plans to come to Haven for an undetermined amount of time in the winter?* The last *city gal* who came to Haven a while back was now buddy-buddy with Fletcher. They didn't need another troublemaker like Avery Culpepper in town, even if Darcy Hill was pretty and sure to turn men's heads.

Darcy settled herself in the passenger seat of the man's beat-up truck, called her auto service and then put her cell phone in her purse. She patted the soft leather, reassuring herself that her handgun was still inside. Her dad had insisted she bring it on the long road trip. She was twenty-seven and lived in her own house not far from her parents' estate in Alabama, but they still worried about her. She was their only child, adopted when she was a few weeks old. In her heart, Mom and Dad were her true parents. They had even supported her trip to Haven.

"Do you know anyone around here?" the cowboy asked as he started his pickup and pulled onto the highway.

"No." Which was true, but she was hoping to get to know her biological father. She wasn't sure whether she would approach him or not—especially since her birth mother had made it clear that she didn't want to meet Darcy. Being rejected by her twice had been a blow. She didn't want another rejection.

"Most people have a reason to visit Haven."

She warmed her hands near a heat vent in the dashboard that put out an inadequate stream of hot air. "I'm not most people. When I was a child, I wanted to visit every state. I've been in Texas before, but it's so big I felt I needed to divide it into sections to do it justice." All technically true. As they neared Haven, she stared out the side window at the lights from a large antebellum house she knew belonged to her biological father. The private investigator who had located Fletcher Phillips had given her a photo of the man's house, along with other pictures of him. She swung her gaze to Nick, the dim interior lights casting his ruggedly handsome features into the shadows but not concealing the strong slope of his jawline and the broad width of his shoulders. "Now that place makes me feel right at home. Who lives there?"

Nick tensed, his shoulders squaring. "Fletcher Phillips."

His stern tone sent up red flags. "I get the impression you don't care for the man. What does he do for a living?" She already knew that but didn't want to appear suspicious.

"A lawyer," he spat out as though it were a dirty word.

"You don't like lawyers or just Fletcher Phillips?" A hard edge entered her words. She'd met her share of people who didn't like any attorney until they needed one. She worked as one for Legal Aid.

"Not this one. He butts his nose in a situation he shouldn't but ignores family members he should take care of."

Darcy swallowed hard, her hand curling around the door handle. Had she made a mistake looking for Fletcher Phillips? Or catching a ride with Nick McGarrett? "Family members?"

Nick slid a glance at her. "You caught me at the wrong time. I just had a run-in with the man over helping his cousins."

Although she couldn't see his face completely, she sensed a softness in his expression. "Cousins?" Before coming to Haven, she'd investigated only her biological father, not anyone else who might be kin to her in this area. Now she wished she had dug a little deeper. She was curious about these other relatives. "Why do they need help?"

"Ned Phillips, Fletcher's cousin, has no business being a father, especially to a young boy."

Her curiosity grew. "Why?" Maybe she should leave now. No, she hadn't come all this way to leave because of Nick's opinion of Fletcher. There were always two sides to a situation. But she made a note to be more cautious about approaching Fletcher.

"Ned has a son, who he neglects—even leaves him alone, usually to go out to drink. Corey is only ten and shouldn't have to take care of himself. I've tried to get Fletcher to at least help the boy."

"And this Fletcher won't?" Obviously it had been a good choice to come to town and scout the situation out first before she said anything to Fletcher Phillips—if she ever did. She wanted information, not a father. She already had a wonderful dad who loved her.

"It's not his problem, according to Fletcher."

So Fletcher doesn't care about family? Darcy's stomach tightened into a knot. She'd known from an early age that she was adopted but always felt as if she were Mom and Dad's real daughter. They had never treated her any other way. So why set herself up for another disappointment by her birth parents?

"But Corey is your problem?" A lump lodged in her throat as she said the boy's name. She'd dealt with enough legal cases that involved children, and she always fought for what was right for them. One day she hoped to have her own kids, and she wouldn't abandon them the way her biological parents had. Although she had had a wonderful childhood with a loving, caring mom and dad, it looked like it could have been just as easily the opposite if she hadn't been put up for adoption.

For a long moment silence reigned in the truck. Then the blare of a country and western song resounded through the cab.

Nick glanced down to see who was calling, and then he pulled over to the side of the road and answered it. "Mrs. Scott, is something wrong?"

The worry in his voice drew Darcy's full attention. As he listened to the person who had called him, his features slashed into a frown. Something bad had happened. Who was Mrs. Scott?

"I'll be right there. I'm glad the police are at Ned's."

When he disconnected, Darcy asked, "What's wrong?"

"Corey is missing. I need to go and help look for him."

Her cousin was missing! She couldn't walk away from an opportunity to meet and help a relative, especially a ten-year-old boy. And it didn't hurt that she would be with Nick McGarrett, an attractive—and caring—cowboy. "Let's go. I'll help."

Chapter Two

"Why do you want to help?" This was the last thing he thought Darcy Hill would offer. "I'm only ten minutes away from the Blue Bonnet Inn. You said you were tired and hungry." Nick gripped the steering wheel and stared at Darcy in the dim light from his dashboard. He couldn't believe he'd told her so much about Corey's situation, but after his meeting with Fletcher today, frustration churned his gut.

"Because a child is missing on a cold winter's night. You'll need everyone you can get to search for him. I couldn't go to the inn without trying to help."

The worry in her expression lured Nick. She showed more feelings toward an unknown kid than Ned did toward his son. Her caring nature appealed to him and made it easy to talk to her.

"Corey lives in Dry Gulch. It might take a long time if we can't find him right away."

"I don't care. A child is in trouble."

Her words touched a cold place in Nick's heart, forged from years living with an alcoholic father like Corey's, and calmed his earlier anger at Fletcher. "You can't go looking for him in what you're wearing." He couldn't believe he was arguing with her about helping Corey. She was right. In the dark, it would be doubly hard to find the child. Did he have a coat on? Did he run away or had something else happened?

"I have some boots in one of my bags. It won't take me long to change into them." She gave him a smile. "I should have when I stopped in Houston and heard the weather report about the cold front moving through this part of Texas."

"Fine. I can't guarantee how long this will take." Nick made another U-turn and headed out of town. He handed her his cell phone. "Slim's number is in my contact list. You can call him and have him tow your car to his garage, and then you can check with him tomorrow morning about what's wrong with it." He shot her another look before pressing on the accelerator. "That way your car will be moved off the shoulder of the highway."

"Thanks. Do you have the number for the

Blue Bonnet Inn? I'd like to tell the owner I'll be late."

"Under Carol Thornton. I've got to warn you, she'll ask a ton of questions about why you'll be late."

"I guess she'll think it's strange I'm helping out."

"No. She's one who will jump in when someone is in trouble, whether she knows the person or not. If I had the time, I would recruit her and a few others. Most townspeople are like family." He increased his speed outside of Haven, pushing the limit.

"Except for Fletcher Phillips?"

"You pick up fast. I won't bother calling him to let him know Corey is missing." Nick tossed a glance at Darcy as a car came toward his truck. Her blond hair hung in thick waves about her shoulders while her blue eyes held a frown. "I hope you have a hat to wear."

"A cowboy one like yours?"

"Nope. A warm one like a beanie."

"Yes, I do, and gloves." She studied the list of contacts on his phone and then connected with one of them.

While she called Slim and Carol, Nick focused on the last twelve miles to Corey's house. The unknown ate at Nick the whole way to Dry Gulch. Nick kept replaying his promise to Doug to keep his little brother safe. When he made a promise, he kept it. What if he couldn't now?

When Darcy finished talking to Carol, she gave him his phone back. "You're right. She drilled me with questions, most of which I couldn't answer. I have a feeling when I finally show up at the inn, I'll have to tell her everything we did."

"I guarantee you will. Carol is like a mother hen."

"Does she have children of her own?"

"No, but not from want of trying. It's a shame. She would have been a great mother."

"I'm assuming Corey doesn't have a mother around since you've only mentioned his dad. Do you know what happened to her?"

"She died years ago."

"That's sad." Her voice caught on her words, and Nick chanced another look at Darcy. Her forehead knit into a thoughtful expression. "Did Mrs. Scott tell you the details of Corey's disappearance?" she finally asked, her tone still emotion-filled.

"Not a lot. Usually Corey will call me, and we'll talk. Mrs. Scott lives next door to Corey and keeps an eye out for the child. All I really know is that Corey is gone and a deputy sheriff is at Ned's house." No doubt Ned had gone out to get some more liquor.

"So he was staying home alone?"

"Most likely." His own feelings warred inside him—from anger at himself for not going earlier, to fear. Apprehension won out. Why didn't Corey call him again instead of running away? What if he couldn't find the boy? "I don't know anything else. Mrs. Scott didn't go into a lot of details. The neighbors are forming a search party to help the deputy. We can join them." Hopefully he'd find out more when he arrived in Dry Gulch. Better yet, maybe Corey was already home and safe.

Nearing the town, Nick slanted another glance toward Darcy, her hands clasped together as though she were praying. It wouldn't help. He'd tried that. Nick had given up on the Lord answering his prayers. At least Ned so far hadn't physically harmed Corey, but neglect of a child was a form of abuse. Corey hungered for love and acceptance.

"We're almost there. Ned and I have exchanged a few words concerning Corey, but nothing will keep me away. I promised Doug, Corey's older brother, that I would watch out for him. I just wanted to let you know things could get tense."

"Does Ned know about what Doug asked you to do?"

Nick turned down a street on the outskirts of

Dry Gulch, a town about the size of Haven. "Yes, and he isn't too happy about that." He pulled behind a long line of cars crammed into every parking spot available. A few floodlights illuminated the area as though it were daytime. "It looks like a lot of people are here. Good. Corey could be in town somewhere, in the woods or on a ranch nearby. Lots of hiding places, and with the darkness he'll be harder to find."

"So you think he's hiding, not taken by someone?" Darcy asked as she opened the passenger door.

"More likely hiding or running away." He hoped. The alternative was even worse. When he hopped down and looked over the hood of his truck at Darcy, he was glad she'd come with him. Although he barely knew Darcy, her presence comforted him. Her immediate response to his news earlier had been to help. There was more to her than too many clothes and shoes. She might come from money, but she didn't act like a spoiled socialite.

He waited for her to join him and then he made his way toward the group of people on the front lawn of Corey's home. Mrs. Scott stood near Ned, talking to him as more neighbors joined the throng. The furious expression on Ned's face alerted Nick that the man probably hadn't been the one who'd called the sheriff's office.

Mrs. Scott saw him and came toward Nick. "We've searched the neighborhood and there wasn't any sign of Corey. We're reorganizing to cover the areas away from here. The sheriff is arriving soon and some more deputies. They're bringing in a couple of tracking dogs too. Five to six inches of snow are predicted tonight. We need to find him before he freezes."

"What happened?" Nick stared at Ned.

"After you called me earlier to check on Ned and Corey, which I did, I left Corey's house because Ned woke up and assured me he was fine. He practically kicked me out. I decided then to make some cookies to share with Corey and Ned as an excuse to check on them after an hour and a half. When I went over to the house, Ned finally opened the door. He looked like he had just woken up, so he'd probably continued to drink after I left. At least that's how he smelled. He invited me in while he called Corey. The boy never came. I helped Ned search his house to make sure Corey wasn't hiding. That man was getting madder by the second. I discovered just a few minutes ago Ned went to the store not long after I left the first time."

Nick swung his attention to Mrs. Scott. "The liquor store?"

Mrs. Scott nodded.

"Are you the one who called the sheriff?"

"Yes. Ned didn't want to. He was sure Corey would show up. By that time it was getting dark. I went home and called."

Nick nodded toward Darcy. "Mrs. Scott, this is Darcy—a friend who heard about Corey and wanted to help."

Darcy shook Mrs. Scott's hand. "I wish we were meeting under better circumstances. Where do you think Corey would have gone?"

"He isn't at any of his friends' houses. The deputy checked those first, so I don't know." Mrs. Scott patted Nick's arm. "If anyone can find him, it's you. I don't know any of his favorite haunts and neither does his father." Anger infused the last sentence. "I declare I haven't seen a man quite like that one."

A conversation Nick had had with Corey last month came to the foreground of his thoughts. The child had been so mad at his father for forgetting to pick him up at his friend's house. He'd ended up walking home. Since it was getting dark, he had used the woods as a shortcut and stumbled upon a thicket—a great hiding place, according to Corey. "There are a few places that Corey and I have talked about. A couple we've been to. But one he said was his secret fort. He told me the general location in the woods. I think we should look there first." Nick didn't want to stand around while the deputies organized the search.

Mrs. Scott's mouth pinched into a frown. "But it's so dark at this time of night. How are you going to look there?"

"I have some flashlights, one in my glove compartment and another in my toolbox. That's all I need." He turned to Darcy and added, "But you might want to stay here—"

"I'm game. It's getting colder." Darcy shivered. "I won't be surprised if there's snow in the next hour or two. We need to find Corey."

"Mrs. Scott, please tell the deputy where we're going and that we could use more people. It's the wooded area behind the elementary school." It would be better if Nick didn't go near Ned at the moment. He threw one last look at the man, who was still frowning as if this whole affair was an inconvenience. Although Nick's and Corey's situations were different, Nick knew the emotional whirlwind the boy was going through and how alone the child must feel.

"Will do, but, dearie," Mrs. Scott said, peering at Darcy's high heels, "you can't go in those shoes."

Darcy grinned. "I'm going to change."

As Nick and Darcy headed for his pickup, she said, "I think you and Mrs. Scott are right—

Corey's dad has been drinking a lot. His eyes are bloodshot, his hands are shaking and his skin is pasty. In my job I've encountered enough alcoholics to know when I see one."

Nick opened the passenger door. "It's been getting worse. That may be what made Corey leave." When his own dad drank, all Nick had wanted to do as a child was hide. He shut the truck door, made his way to the driver's side and switched on the engine, throwing a glance at Darcy. "What's your job?"

For a long moment Darcy didn't answer. Nick turned the truck around and headed the way they had come. Still no reply.

He was about to tell her to forget the question when she murmured, "I'm a lawyer—for Legal Aid."

Surprise flitted through him. He wasn't sure what he'd pictured her doing. When he thought about it, the fact that she was a lawyer wasn't what astonished him—it was that she worked for Legal Aid. The clothes she wore and the car she drove didn't fit his image of the belongings of someone working for the poor. And yet, she'd quickly volunteered to search for a child she didn't know. He was discovering there was a lot under the cool, composed facade she presented to the world.

"You can close your mouth now. I've been

working at the office in Mobile since I got out of law school a few years ago. My father comes from old money. Giving back to the community is very important to both my parents. When I was young, no more than five, he had me volunteering right alongside him or my mother. By the time I went to college I knew I was going to fight for people who often can't fight for themselves."

"You need to give Fletcher Phillips a lesson in how to give back. Instead, he pushes his own agenda to make more money."

"Are you talking about Ned and Corey?"

"Yes, that's one example, but the boys ranch is another."

"What boys ranch?"

"We have a Lone Star Cowboy League Boys Ranch here in Haven, founded in 1947 by Luella Snowden Phillips. She used her own ranch as a place for troubled boys around the state to receive support and care and to learn a better way to deal with their problems."

"Any relative to Fletcher Phillips?"

"Yes, his grandmother. But he wants to close the place down."

"Why would he want to shut down something his grandmother started and supported?"

"Good question. Now you see why he isn't one of my favorite people. He says it devalues the property around the boys ranch and hurts

Haven's economy. All he sees is a bunch of troublemakers, not young children and teens who have problems. His father, Tucker, was actively involved in the ranch. He isn't alive, but if he were he would be so disappointed in his son."

"I can see why you feel that way about Fletcher, but has anyone invited him to the ranch to see firsthand what's going on? Maybe even volunteer and get to know the children?"

Had they? Nick didn't know. "The townspeople are always welcomed at the boys ranch."

"Sometimes the obvious has to be pointed out to some people."

Nick chuckled. "That would be Fletcher, but I can't see even a grand tour of the boys ranch changing that man's mind. And I certainly can't see him volunteering there." He pulled into a parking space at the elementary school. "I met my share of people in the army who had to have it their way or no way. They were rigid and never wanted to compromise."

"There are people like that in every facet of life. I try to look at things from their perspective."

Nick climbed from the truck, paused and asked over the hood, "How's that working for you?"

"Actually pretty well, but I'll admit there are some who can make it hard for a person."

Nick studied her profile as she stared at the woods across the field. Was he one of those people? The thought didn't sit well with him. "So why do you think Ned drinks himself into a stupor and ignores his son?"

"I imagine the second part comes because of the first—Ned's drinking problem. Most people drink to excess because they aren't happy and don't know how to make it better. What happened to Corey's mother?"

Nick walked to the back of the truck and let the tailgate down. "I don't know. Corey was a toddler when she died. He said his dad wouldn't talk about her." And that topic never came up with his army buddy, Corey's older brother. Her question brought thoughts up about Nick's own mother, who died when he was seven. Was that what led to his father's drinking problem? Even so, that didn't give him the right to hit Nick whenever he felt like it. He was thankful that by the time he was fifteen his dad had backed off. Probably because Nick was stronger and bigger than his father.

He gestured to her multiple bags. "Which one do you need?"

Darcy pointed to two of them, and Nick slid them to her. "Maybe Corey running away will shake up his dad," she said as she changed her shoes and found her hat and gloves.

Nick shut the tailgate, handed her a flashlight and then started across the school playground toward the woods. "Probably not. This isn't the first time he's gone missing, but usually the sheriff isn't involved. No doubt he is this time because Mrs. Scott knew something was wrong and called them. Ned never would have. I don't know what would have happened if Mrs. Scott didn't help me out by keeping an eye on the boy. If she hadn't come back with cookies, Ned would have resumed drinking and still might have been oblivious to the fact that Corey could be freezing to death."

"Did you know Doug before y'all were in the army?"

He switched on his flashlight, the crunch of fallen leaves sounding in the quiet. "Yes, the family lived in Haven for a while when I was a freshman in high school. That's when Doug and I became friends. Then his family left and went to Dry Gulch. When I enlisted, I met up with Doug again at boot camp. He was escaping his father like I was." The last sentence came out before he could censor himself. Darcy was too easy to talk to.

"You were?"

He didn't share his past with anyone. Even he and Uncle Howard didn't talk much about what had happened as Nick grew up. It just brought up hard feelings toward his dad, and Nick had enough to deal with keeping the ranch afloat due to his father's mismanagement. Nick had used all his savings to bail the Flying Eagle out of debt, but he didn't have enough left to do much else. "I was a teenage boy who thought he knew what was best for him."

"Where is Doug now?"

"He was killed on a mission."

Darcy slowed her step. "I'm sorry to hear that. I see why you're trying to help Corey."

Frustration at his inability to help Corey as much as the kid needed plagued Nick. It brought back all the helplessness he'd felt as a child.

As they moved deeper into the stand of trees, Darcy followed a step or two behind, sweeping her flashlight over the left area while Nick searched the right side.

She'd never imagined she would be spending her first night in Haven looking for a lost child. But there was no way she would have stayed away. Corey and she were kin.

Family had always been important to her—something she didn't take for granted. What if her mom and dad hadn't adopted her? Then where would she be? Until she'd begun the search for her biological parents, she hadn't really thought much about where she'd come from. When her birth mother rejected the offer to meet with her, it had devastated her more than she thought possible. And after hearing about Fletcher, she didn't think meeting her birth father would be any different. The thought saddened her.

She shouldn't unpack. Instead, she should just leave when her car was fixed. She should forget the father who had never cared for her—and, from what she was discovering about the man, would never care in the future. He'd turned his back on a ten-year-old cousin. She always tried to look for the good in others, but with each bit of information she found out about her father, it was becoming more difficult. *Lord, how could Fletcher Phillips do that to a child—in fact, to a whole ranch full of boys in need?*

She didn't realize she had slowed her step until suddenly Nick was several yards in front of her. She hurried her pace and the toe of her boot caught on a root, throwing her off balance. She floundered and nearly fell.

But Nick grabbed her, halting her ungraceful descent. "You okay?" He steadied her, close enough that she got a good whiff of his citrus-scented aftershave.

Her heartbeat picked up speed. "I tripped. That's all." She needed to keep her thoughts centered on finding Corey, not why she came to Haven—or the man she was with. There was something about Nick—the way he talked about Corey—that attracted her.

Her breathing shortened. He was too close for her peace of mind. "Thanks." She stepped back and inhaled deeply. "Are we near the place Corey was talking about?" she asked, wanting to focus on the child, not the racing of her heartbeat. "I noticed a few snowflakes falling."

"I know. His fort should be up ahead. I just hope he's there. If not, I'll call Mrs. Scott and see if Corey has been found."

"What if he hasn't been?"

"Then I think we really need to comb these woods. He uses it as a shortcut from school as well as to his friend's house. It'll be harder in the dark. We'll need a lot more people. I'm glad they're using some tracking dogs. In the meantime, we can at least rule out his fort and this part of the forest."

Darcy scanned the towering trees, some leafless, others evergreens or ones that retain their dead leaves until spring. A black veil dominated the area beyond the glow of their flashlights. She quaked. "I guess for a boy this would be a great place to play in during the daytime." *But not at night.*

"But not for a girl?" Nick continued forward, glancing back to make sure she was behind him.

Even from a distance she sensed the concern that gripped him.

"No, for some it would be. Not for me though. I wasn't much of a tomboy, except when it came to fishing. I love to go fishing. My dad owned a boat, and we often went out in the Gulf of Mexico. So much fun. What did you do for fun growing up?" Maybe concentrating on something other than Corey's predicament would reduce Nick's stress. She'd learned in her work that tension only made a situation worse, sometimes leading to bad decisions.

"I played football and baseball. I was also part of the junior rodeo."

"I took ballet and played the violin. I did learn to ride a horse English-style." As a teen she gave up the other two interests to focus on her mare and going to horse shows.

"We come from different worlds."

The more she was around him, the more she realized that, and yet there was something about Nick that intrigued her. He'd made a promise to a comrade to take care of his little brother, and he was determined to keep it. Like her, he fought for the underdog. She admired him for that. For that matter, he'd stopped to help her when her car died even though he was going the other way.

Finally Nick halted and pointed to a large thicket of bushes up ahead. "That's the fort," he said and then he called out loudly, "Corey, it's Nick."

Darcy held her breath. *Please, Lord, let him be here and okay.*

Nothing but the sound of the wind blowing through the woods.

Nick closed the distance between them and the dense undergrowth. "Corey, I want to help."

"I'm glad it's cold enough that things like snakes are hibernating," Darcy said as they approached.

"So am I."

"Are you scared of snakes?"

"Nope. But we have a lot of rattlers around here, and I don't want Corey to encounter one. Oh, and by the way, snakes don't hibernate. I've seen some in the winter." He winked and then started to the side. "You stay here. I'm gonna circle this brush and see if there's an easy way in."

Oh, good. He'd said that bit about the snakes on purpose and then left. She scowled at his back. As Nick moved farther away, Darcy hugged her chest and tried to see through the green-and-brown barrier in front of her where she was shining her flashlight. What if a rattlesnake was keeping warm under the thicket—and Corey had been bitten by it? What if…

Darcy quickly shut down those thoughts. She liked frills and lace. She liked girly things, and a snake wasn't one of those. She and Nick were definitely opposites and that was fine by her. And yet, she remembered his quick reflexes when he caught her before she could hit the ground. Okay, they might be opposites, but there was an appeal to the cowboy who dropped everything to look for a child.

Whoa. Where were these thoughts coming from? Exhaustion after driving all day? She wasn't in Haven for anything but gathering information about her birth father. She was going to be here only a short time. The more she heard about Fletcher the less she wanted to talk to him, but it wouldn't be right to pass up discovering what she could about her biological family since she wanted children of her own.

To her left Nick shouted, "Stop, Corey!"

The next thing Darcy saw was the boy rounding the end of the undergrowth, coming to a halt when he spied her and then darting to the side to avoid her. Nick closed in on him from behind. Darcy shot forward, trying to block his escape. When she was within a few feet of him, she took a flying leap and tackled Corey to the ground.

"Get off me! Get off me!" the child yelled.

Still clutching her flashlight, Darcy threw her body across his stomach while Corey wiggled and twisted. Was this what riding a wild bronco felt like?

Through her strands of blond hair she saw two cowboy boots planted near Corey's shoulder, a pool of light coming no doubt from Nick's flashlight. She thought it was safe for her to sit up, but the second she did, the boy jumped to his feet and tried to race away.

With lightning speed Nick grasped the child's upper arms and held him still. "What's going on with you, Corey?"

"I don't want to go back. I'll run away again if you make me go."

The anger in the boy's voice made Darcy forget about the dead leaves clinging to her coat and the bruises she was sure to develop from stopping him. Beneath his fury was desperation. She'd heard it enough in her job at Legal Aid. Not long after desperation came hopelessness. She tried to stop that from being someone's reality. Who was going to give Corey hope? His father? Not unless something changed.

Corey tried to yank his arms away from Nick, tears running down his face now.

All Darcy wanted to do was hold the boy until he calmed down, but she couldn't, even though he was her cousin—family. Besides Fletcher, she was probably his closest relative in the area. But no one knew that but her.

"Let me go. Dad doesn't care." A sob caught in Corey's throat.

Nick still held Corey, but when he knelt in front of the boy, his expression softened. "But I care about you. It's gonna snow and get really cold tonight. Did you think about that?"

Corey looked to the side. His blue gaze—so much like Darcy's—landed on her. "Who are you?"

The words *I'm your cousin* almost slipped out. Instead she smiled and said, "I want to help you."

"You can't. No one can."

The hopelessness leaked into his words and broke her heart. Coming to Haven was so much harder than Darcy had ever thought it would be.

"That's not going to stop me from trying. I don't know about you, Corey, but Miss Hill and I are cold. Let's settle this somewhere warm."

Her cousin stuck out his lower lip. "Fine. Nothing's gonna change."

"There are a lot of people searching for you and worried about you. Mrs. Scott was beside herself. She called the sheriff." Nick kept his hand clamped on Corey's shoulder and started back toward the elementary school parking lot.

"Dad will be mad about that."

"What did you think was going to happen if you ran away?" Darcy boxed the boy in on the other side and prepared to go after him if he broke loose from Nick's hold.

"Somethin' better. Anywhere would be better than here," Corey mumbled and dropped his head as he shuffled his feet toward the edge of the woods.

When Darcy returned to Mobile, the first thing she would do was hug her parents. She knew raising kids was difficult, but seeing someone like Corey only made her want to have her own children more than before. She had so much love to give a child.

She'd been blessed to have a wonderful mother and father. But others, like Corey, hadn't been. Maybe while she stayed in Haven, she would check out the boys ranch. Her biological father might not want to have anything to do with the place, but she did.

The minute they returned to Nick's truck, he settled Corey inside. While the boy sat sandwiched between them, Nick called Mrs. Scott to let her know they had found Corey.

The child folded his arms over his chest and hunched his shoulders farther down as Nick drove closer to Corey's house. In that moment Darcy felt like a fish in the Gulf taking the bait and being caught. It would be hard to drive home to Mobile without making sure something long term was done for Corey. The question was what. Nick, one of the few people who cared for the child and the person who had stopped to help her tonight, might be able to assist her with that.

Chapter Three

Darcy didn't even know Corey, and still she wanted to do everything she could to take care of him. Make sure he was warm and fed a proper meal. There was something about the child that drew her—more than family ties. There was a lot of anger in Corey, but beneath it she sensed a need to be loved, or maybe she was just putting herself in Corey's situation and projecting her emotions onto him.

As they drove away from Dry Gulch, where they'd left Corey with the neighbor, Darcy turned to Nick. "Where I live, I volunteer at a shelter and work with children to find solutions for their situations. I've seen families deal with a member who is an alcoholic and the toll it puts on them, especially the children. Some of the kids have to grow up so fast because they are left to fend for themselves. It breaks my heart."

Nick waited at a stoplight to turn onto the highway that would return them to Haven. He slid a look at her, his expression still full of worry. “Me too.” Unspoken emotions dripped from those brief words.

“What do you think will happen to Ned?” Darcy asked the question she was sure was on both their minds. They had left Dry Gulch after the sheriff arrested Ned and hauled him to jail.

“He’ll probably only get a slap on the wrist. I’m more concerned about Corey. At least he’s with Mrs. Scott for the night.”

“Are you upset that Ned wouldn’t let you take Corey home?”

Nick gave her a tired smile. “Am I that transparent?”

“Well…yes.”

“Ned doesn’t want to be the father he should, but he feels threatened by my relationship with Corey. I’m glad Ned let Mrs. Scott take Corey without much of a fight. She’ll take good care of the child, and I’ll go to her house tomorrow morning.”

“But you wanted to take him home.”

“Yes, I feel responsible for him,” Nick said, although she hadn’t asked a question.

“Because of the promise to Doug?”

“Yep. When I give my word, I mean it. But it’s more than…” Nick’s voice trailed off in silence.

"He'll be all right. I'm glad she called the sheriff earlier. All Corey had with him was a thin blanket. He could have frozen tonight."

There was something Nick wasn't saying. What? "Ned could be looking at child endangerment and neglect. The state could step in."

"I hope they do something this time."

"What do you mean, *this time*?"

"I have reported Ned's behavior before, but nothing was done. He left Corey alone overnight. Corey called me afraid because he heard a noise outside. I came over to be with him until his dad showed up in the morning. That's when my precarious relationship with Ned turned from bad to worse. Thankfully Mrs. Scott has been able to step in more, but she's had health issues. She's a temporary solution but not a permanent one."

"How about the boys ranch for Corey?"

"I know they have room for one more boy, and I'd much rather see Corey there, but Ned would never go for it."

"Unless this time the state does something about it."

"I volunteer at the boys ranch, and it's done a lot for the kids who live there. I'm there several times a week. It would be so much better for Corey than living with Ned. The boys ranch isn't like what Fletcher says. They aren't hooligans but kids who need extra help."

She wasn't surprised that Nick would volunteer at the boys ranch. In the short time she'd been with him, she'd seen a man of action and heart. "Then I'll pray to the Lord something is done for Corey."

"In my experience He hasn't helped much."

There was something in Nick's voice—pain—that touched her. Who did he turn to when he was in trouble or upset? She started to say something in reply to Nick's last statement, but the tense set of his jaw and rigid posture indicated this wasn't a good time. He wouldn't hear her.

She didn't want to leave Haven until something was done for Corey. How could she walk away from a child in need, a child she was related to?

She relished the silence as Nick drove toward Haven. Exhaustion weaved through her body, and she had to fight to keep her eyes open. But she perked up when he neared the place where her car had stalled. "Good. Slim must have towed my car."

"He'll be able to give you an estimate for fixing the car early tomorrow morning."

"I hope he can fix it right away." She only had a few weeks to discover what she'd come for, and after what Nick had told her about Fletcher trying to shut down the boys ranch, she wanted to see it too.

"At least the Blue Bonnet Inn is near downtown and within walking distance of most places, but Slim is gifted when repairing anything with a motor. The only thing that will hold him back is if he has to order a part. We don't have too many suppliers in this area, but Waco will."

Nick parked in front of a three-story Victorian house with a sign saying Blue Bonnet Inn. Lights illuminated the long, partial-wraparound porch and its white wicker furniture. Darcy's first thought was that it looked inviting, homey and peaceful. A perfect place to take her long-overdue, four-week vacation. She hadn't realized how much she needed to take a break until this moment. She sighed.

"Ready? Knowing Carol, she'll be up waiting for you." Nick assessed her.

And usually when someone did, it made Darcy uncomfortable, but she must be too tired to even feel that. "It's eleven. A lot has happened today."

"More than you bargained for, but I appreciate your help."

"Anytime. I hope you'll let me know what happens with Corey."

"Yes, ma'am, just as soon as I know." Nick tipped the brim of his cowboy hat and then climbed from his truck.

Darcy did the same and grabbed some of the luggage he'd put on the ground near the tailgate. When he hefted the two bigger suitcases as well as her duffel bag, he looked loaded down but strong enough to manage. Yesterday when she'd packed, she hadn't known what she would do once she came to Haven, so she'd planned for everything she could think of. Now she realized it appeared she was moving in rather than staying for a short vacation.

Darcy started for the entrance to the inn with her hands full too. "When I was trying to figure out what to bring, I read that the weather here can be spring-like one day and full winter the next."

"So you brought all your clothes?" He paused on the porch, the bright light allowing her a good look at Nick McGarrett.

He was mighty attractive. "No, I left more than half my wardrobe behind."

"You're kidding?"

"I'm afraid not. I like clothes but especially shoes. The duffel bag is full of them."

He shook his head and moved toward the front door. "I own a pair of tennis shoes and dress boots as well as work ones. That's all."

Over six foot three, he commanded a confident presence. His chestnut-brown hair peeked out from under his cowboy hat. She would have been able to tell his build was muscular even if she hadn't known one suitcase was full of books she'd wanted to read but had been too busy to this past year. The angular planes of his face complemented his firm mouth, but what drew her full attention were his piercing blue eyes, reminding her of the Gulf on a sunny day.

"Men don't have all the choices women have," she finally said when she realized she was staring at him and he'd noticed.

"Don't see a need for so many choices. Makes getting dressed much easier."

The heat of a blush flooded her face. She opened the door and stepped into the inn, the scent of lavender filling the air and welcoming her in from the cold. Ah, someone who understood the importance of essential oils. Already she was letting go of her stress.

Darcy scanned the large foyer, glimpsing into a dining room on one side and a large living room on the other. Antiques, such as a bookcase, desk and end tables, were sprinkled among the elegant but comfortable-looking couches and chairs. She took a step toward what must be the heart of the inn, enthralled by the beautifully carved mahogany coffee table between two cream-colored sofas.

A middle-aged woman with auburn hair pulled into a bun came from the back of the house. "You must be Darcy Hill. I'm so glad you're here. I'm Carol Thornton, the owner of the Blue Bonnet Inn." Her eyes crinkled at the corners when she smiled.

Darcy immediately felt at home. "Yes, I am. You have a beautiful place."

"It's been in my family for years." Carol turned to Nick. "How's Corey?"

"Safe and staying with Mrs. Scott, his neighbor. The sheriff arrested Ned."

"It's about time they did something about that man's neglect and drinking. If I can help, let me know, Nick," Carol said, then shifted her gaze back to Darcy. "I called Slim, and he has your car. He'll look at it first thing in the morning."

"That'll be great. Nick told me I could walk to the garage."

Carol waved her hand. "It's only a few blocks away, but then a lot of places are here in Haven. If you need a ride, I can help or my husband, Clarence, can. Speaking of my husband, he fell asleep an hour ago. He's been fighting a migraine all day. Will you please—"

"Say no more, Carol. Where do you want me to take these suitcases?" Nick, still loaded down with Darcy's bags, walked to the staircase. "Then I need to leave. Tomorrow will be here soon enough."

"The second room on the right. Thank you, Nick. I knew I could count on you."

"And I can take care of these." Darcy gestured to the few she'd set on the floor. Before Carol could say anything, Darcy picked up the bags and mounted the stairs behind Nick.

"Are you hungry?"

Darcy paused halfway up and looked down at Carol. "Starving."

"When you're settled, come down to the kitchen. I'll fix you and Nick bowls of vegetable soup to tide you over until morning."

"Thanks. It sounds delicious." If she had the energy even to eat.

Darcy continued to trudge up the stairs, her body protesting with each step. When she reached the second floor, she noticed the door to the second room on the right was open. Nick came out of the entrance and retrieved two pieces of luggage from her.

"You look like you're on your last leg." He disappeared into her room.

How did he still have so much energy? She'd left hers back in Dry Gulch after getting Corey into Nick's truck. Once they'd found the child, what she'd been functioning on drained from her quickly.

The second she moved into her suite all she wanted to do was go to sleep. Suddenly, not even food was enough to motivate her to go back downstairs.

"Will you please tell Carol that I've changed my mind? If I made it downstairs, I know I wouldn't make it up here again. And I doubt she would want a guest sleeping on a couch in her living room."

He stopped in front of her and removed the remaining bags from her grasp. His eyes locked with hers. "I know how you feel. I've been running on adrenaline the past few hours, and now I don't have any left. I'll tell her and let you know when I hear something about Corey."

Fighting the urge to lose herself in his blue gaze, she was surprised she had the energy even to smile, but she managed somehow. She didn't look away. "I appreciate that."

For a long moment he remained in front of her. She couldn't move. Nick attracted her. She didn't know a lot about him personally, but she'd seen him in action tonight, trying to find a child. Too bad she wouldn't be here more than three or four weeks before she returned to Alabama and her life there.

For the past two years, she'd been dating a guy who worked with her at the Legal Aid office in Mobile. They had so much in common—helping others, the same career—and she'd known him for years, but right before the holidays, they had mutually decided to be only friends. There was no spark between them, and she was beginning to believe there never would be.

She needed to focus on what she came to do, not a cowboy who made her start questioning her love life—or lack of one. She was just passing through Haven, here to learn about Fletcher and now any other family members. Then she would leave.

Nick strolled past Darcy and out into the hall. He gave her one nod. His actions dragged her away from her perfectly happy life in Alabama. Their gazes connected one last time. Her pulse sped while her lungs held her breath.

"Again, thanks for your help this evening. Good night." His deep, husky voice wrapped around her, chasing away any lingering chill from earlier and confusing her even more.

The sound of his footsteps going down the stairs echoed through her mind until she finally shook herself out of her daze, plodded to the four-poster bed and collapsed on it. Her last thought as sleep descended was of Nick holding Corey as he tried to console the boy. He would make a great father.

After feeding the animals the next morning, Nick entered his house through the back door, stomping off the snow that had fallen lightly throughout the night. At least Darcy was comfortable at the inn and Corey was with Mrs. Scott. Nick would drive over to Dry Gulch after he ate breakfast. Then he could hopefully let Darcy know what would happen with Corey.

The events of the day before only reconfirmed he wouldn't be a good father. Yes, he had found Corey, but he should have been there in the first place and stopped the child before he ran away.

Nick hung his overcoat and Stetson on a peg, noticing a beige hat and a black jacket on the remaining two hooks. The ever-present scent of coffee peppered the air. He loved that smell. The sound of shuffling footsteps coming toward the kitchen alerted him to his uncle's presence.

"I didn't hear you come in last night or get up this morning. I tried to stay up, but obviously I fell asleep in my lounge chair. You should have awakened me. How's Corey?"

"We found him." Nick went on to tell his uncle about Ned's arrest and Mrs. Scott taking the boy.

"I figured he was okay or you wouldn't have come home. What's this about you picking up a stranger?" His uncle, a tall, thin man with graying hair, ambled to the refrigerator, removed a mixing bowl and poured its contents into a black skillet on the stove.

"How did you hear about Darcy?"

"Carol called me to let me know what was

happening in case you forgot to. Of course, she knows you would have filled me in eventually. It was just an excuse to gossip, although she didn't tell me a lot about this woman you rescued on the highway."

"I don't know a lot. She's about my age. She's a lawyer." He wouldn't tell his uncle how pretty Darcy was or he would make more of it. Uncle Howard was determined Nick would marry one day. Nick was just as resolved to stay single. Even when his mother was alive, his parents' marriage had been volatile—not something he would want.

"Carol told me Darcy has the room booked for three weeks with a possibility of staying a fourth one." Uncle Howard's curiosity came to the forefront of their conversation as he scrambled the eggs and then popped some bread into the toaster. "Why would a young woman come here and stay? We don't have too many coming through here, besides that Avery gal. And Avery has her own agenda."

Nick chuckled. "Don't know why."

His uncle shook his head. "Did you find out anything else about her?"

"I figure Carol and Clarence will get the lowdown and tell you. You three are such gossipers. Darcy is probably being drilled right now by Carol."

Uncle Howard propped one hand on his waist. "I do not gossip. I'm genuinely interested in the people around me."

"And yet you haven't discovered who is sabotaging the boys ranch or, for that matter, who messed with our fence a while back."

"I'm working on it, but I ain't no detective." When two picces of bread popped up lightly toasted, Howard buttered each slice and set it on a plate. "I don't see why anyone would steal children's saddles, especially from a home for troubled boys."

"I could think of one—Fletcher. And the way the man feels about me bothering him about Corey, he could have sabotaged our fence too."

"I've considered him, but he would just use his influence and money to shut down the ranch, not soil his hands taking the saddles or letting the calves loose. Don't quite know why he's so against the ranch when his dad did a lot for it. I'm glad Tucker isn't alive to know what his son is doing. Now, our ranch might be another story. Fletcher ain't too happy with you. When are you going to the boys ranch next?"

"Tomorrow for sure. Flint said there are two horses I need to look at." Nick volunteered as a farrier when they needed one.

"I'm so glad he's found someone. Lana is perfect for him and will be a great mother for Logan."

"Married life will agree with Flint." Left unsaid was that marriage wouldn't work for Nick, especially with someone who wanted children. Seeing what Corey was going through only reinforced that notion.

"It's good for a lot of men. Look at Heath and Josie."

"Stop right there. Flint is the foreman at the boys ranch, and Heath is a Texas Ranger—they do all right for themselves. I'm struggling to make this ranch viable, and I don't know how I could support a wife when this place needs so much. So quit trying to fix me up. I don't have the time."

"There's always Avery Culpepper," Uncle Howard said with a chuckle, while dishing up the scrambled eggs.

Several months ago, Cyrus Culpepper, one of the boys ranch's earliest residents, had died and bequeathed his family place to the Lone Star Cowboy League. The larger property allowed the boys ranch to take in more kids. The only hitch to the inheritance was that the town had to find the four other original residents of the ranch, besides Cyrus. Also Avery Culpepper, Cyrus's granddaughter, needed to be located. And she had been, but Lana didn't think the woman who claimed to be Avery was the real one.

"Do you think she is for real?" Nick asked. If she wasn't, the boys ranch wouldn't meet all the terms of Cyrus's will, and the ranch would be sold to a developer to build a strip mall. The boys would have to be moved again. If that wasn't motivation to find everyone listed in the old man's will, Nick didn't know what was.

"I sure hope she is."

"Avery has been cozy with Fletcher, and he wants the land to be sold."

"I don't see him behind what has been going on at the boys ranch." Uncle Howard placed a plate in front of Nick and then went back and brought the coffeepot to the kitchen table.

"I agree. Stealing a therapy horse and saddles and letting out calves doesn't make sense unless Fletcher has really stooped low and is resorting to these tactics to shut down the boys ranch. He's a lawyer. He'll seek a legal way if he can."

"Fletcher has blinders on to the good the place does for kids who need help. But then the man doesn't have any children." Uncle Howard poured some coffee into his mug and then handed the pot to Nick.

"Neither do I, but I see the benefits of the ranch. He's just plain mean-spirited."

"He never used to bother you so much until you came home and began looking out for Corey."

"How can someone who has plenty of money

turn his back on family? Ned Phillips has no business being a father. No wonder Doug was concerned about Corey." And no wonder Nick never wanted to be a father himself. He didn't have the skills needed to be responsible for someone else.

"You've done what you can. Sometimes we just have to leave it in the Lord's hands."

"And look how well that has worked out," Nick mumbled and drank a mouthful of his coffee.

"I wish I could have done more for you with your father, but I lived so far away. I failed you. I'm sorry."

"You didn't know. He was good at hiding his abusive behavior. Once I tried telling someone, and I learned the hard way to keep my mouth shut. As far as I know, Ned hasn't physically abused Corey, but verbally he tears the boy down all the time. It breaks my heart." Nick's stomach roiled with thoughts of the boy's situation and the reminders of what he had gone through when his father drank.

"That's why I think you'd be a good father. You know what not to do." Then before Nick could reply, Uncle Howard bowed his head and said grace. When he looked up at Nick, he said, "I'm not giving up on you."

"I don't need—"

The ringtone on Nick's cell phone distracted him. Quickly Nick answered, noting it was Mrs. Scott. "Is something wrong with Corey?"

"The state is sending him to the boys ranch. They just came and took him. Corey threatened he would run away again."

Chapter Four

The morning of her second day in Haven, Darcy stood at the inn's front picture window in the living room, holding a warm cup of coffee and staring at the snow-covered street. The snowfall had only been a couple of inches, but for a Southern gal like herself, driving even in a small accumulation made her so nervous she was afraid she would cause an accident. She would stay at the inn or walk to where she wanted to go until the car part came in and Slim installed it, hopefully later this afternoon.

Still, sitting around waiting today made her antsy. Her time here was limited, and after Corey running away last night, she wanted to make sure he would be all right before she left Haven at the end of the month.

She took a sip of her coffee as footfalls sounded on the hardwood floor. When she glanced over her shoulder, Avery Culpepper entered the room. She had long, bouncy blond hair and wore a baby blue wool dress that matched her big eyes and spiked heels, as well as more makeup than Darcy put on in a week. Darcy had met her briefly earlier that morning.

Darcy smiled. "Good morning. Carol will have breakfast ready in five minutes. There's coffee in the dining room."

"I'll get some later." Avery joined Darcy at the window. "Thankfully there wasn't too much snow. I'm meeting Fletcher this morning."

"Fletcher Phillips?"

Avery brushed her hair away from her face. "He's the only Fletcher in this town. He's a lawyer who's been giving me some advice for when I get my inheritance."

"Inheritance?"

"From my grandfather, Cyrus Culpepper."

"The one who bequeathed his land to the boys ranch?"

"Yes." Avery glanced out the window. "I've got to go. See you around."

Darcy watched as Avery headed toward Fletcher's Lexus. He climbed out of the car and rounded the hood to open the passenger door for Avery. Darcy's biological father wore a Stetson, a black suit and boots. She must have gotten her height from him because her birth mother was only five foot two.

He turned his head toward the bed-and-breakfast, and their gazes met and held for a few seconds. Because she was looking for it, she saw a resemblance between them in the eyes and chin. He had a cleft in it like she did. She pivoted away and moved from the window. Her heartbeat thudded against her rib cage.

What was Fletcher Phillips doing with a woman half his age?

She felt as though she'd stepped into the middle of a story and didn't know what had already happened.

"I hope you're hungry. Breakfast is ready," Carol said from the living room entrance.

Darcy blinked and pushed thoughts of Fletcher from her mind. Besides Avery and her, there was only another couple staying at the inn. The husband and wife weren't in the dining room. She was curious about the people of Haven, and from what she'd seen so far, Carol would be a great person to talk to.

"Will you sit and join me? I hate eating alone." Darcy sat at a table for four with a coffeepot and a bread basket already on it.

Carol smiled. "I'd love to. Be right back with our breakfast."

When she disappeared through the door into

the kitchen, Darcy poured herself a cup of coffee and dumped several scoops of sugar into the brew. Carol returned with two plates, placed one in front of Darcy and then took the chair across from her.

Darcy peered at her omelet and the slices of melon on the side. "This looks delicious. I usually don't have much time to eat a big breakfast."

"I have some blueberry and bran muffins in the basket."

"This omelet and fruit is perfect. I stay away from breads."

"You have to watch your weight? You're thin."

"I have celiac disease and have to avoid all foods with gluten in them." When she was diagnosed six months ago, Darcy had begun her search for her biological parents. Celiac was a genctic disorder. Was there anything else she needed to be aware of in her family history?

"Are you all right now?"

Darcy didn't like talking about that time of uncertainty when she didn't know why she was tired all the time, losing weight and getting sick after eating certain foods. "Yes, so long as I follow my diet." She bowed her head and blessed the food.

When she looked up, Carol was studying her. "If you're still here on Sunday, you're welcome to attend the Haven Community Church with me and Clarence."

"I'd love to. What few people I've met so far have been friendly."

"Most are in Haven. There isn't much that goes on in our town that others don't know about."

"Nick mentioned someone called Fletcher Phillips. Do you know him?"

"I imagine Nick wasn't too happy with Fletcher when he talked about him. Nick volunteers at the Lone Star Cowboy League Boys Ranch, and Fletcher is trying to get it shut down."

"Why?" Darcy wanted Carol's take on the boys ranch.

"He thinks having a boys ranch here is bringing down the value of the property around town. All he sees is troublemaking kids. That's really not the case. The children need love and care, but he won't listen to reason."

"How do the people in Haven feel about it?" Darcy ate her first bite of omelet, the taste tempting her to take cooking lessons from Carol.

"Some go along with Fletcher, but there are many who don't."

"What would happen to the boys staying there if he got his way?"

"That would be the state's problem. The ranch

is licensed by the Texas Department of Family and Protective Services for their residential needs and for programs to help the boys."

First from Nick and now from Carol, Darcy wasn't getting a good feeling about her biological father. "Which side of the argument do you support?"

"One hundred percent for the boys ranch. My husband was there for a few years as a kid when his dad died and his mother couldn't manage him. Fletcher thinks of the boys as juvenile delinquents. They are troubled but still children."

As Darcy ate her omelet, she decided she would drive out there and look into the ranch. Without seeing it, she couldn't form an opinion. Did Fletcher have a legitimate concern? "I'd like to see the place, maybe later today if I get my car back. How would the people running it feel if I went to see the ranch?"

"I'm sure Bea Brewster, the director, would welcome you." Carol rose and stacked their plates. "I'll make a map for you. And I'll call her to let her know you're coming by."

As Carol hurried away, Darcy finished the last of her coffee, pleased she had something to do. When she'd planned to come here, she hadn't thought of how she would spend her time other than catching up on her reading. She liked to keep busy, and looking into the boys ranch was a good way to have something to do—and possibly see Nick when he volunteered.

A minute after the phone rang, Carol reappeared in the living room. "Nick's on the phone for you."

"He is?" Darcy followed Carol to the phone in the hallway, surprised to be hearing from him, especially after she had just been thinking of him. When she answered, she asked, "Is Corey okay?"

"Not exactly. I'm at Mrs. Scott's house. The state is taking Corey to the boys ranch, and he's locked himself in the bathroom, screaming he won't go there. Mrs. Scott is looking for the skeleton key."

Her first urge was to drive to Mrs. Scott's house and do…what? She was a relative stranger to Corey. "I wish I could help. My car won't be repaired until late this afternoon or possibly tomorrow. Will he go to the ranch today?"

"Yes. I just wanted to let you know because of your concern last night."

"Thanks. I appreciate it. If I get my car fixed later today, could I visit Corey at the ranch?"

"Seeing someone familiar would be great."

"We don't know each other well, but I'm glad to come as soon as I can."

When Darcy hung up, Carol came over to her. "I couldn't help overhearing that Nick's friend is going to the boys ranch. If you don't get your car back, I'll drive you."

"I couldn't ask you to do that."

"It would be a good reason for me to pay a visit to my friend Bea. I could take you after I do a few things around here."

"Thanks. I'll let you know about my car."

An hour and a half later, Carol drove Darcy to the boys ranch. Carol had called and discovered Corey was there at the barn with Nick. Darcy dressed in jeans, a white blouse and tennis shoes. As she strolled to the porch with Carol, she noticed Nick's beat-up pickup parked next to the barn. Before she had a chance to ring the bell, the front door swung open and an older woman with brown hair and brown eyes appeared in the entrance.

The lady hugged Carol and then turned to Darcy. "It's nice to meet you, Darcy." She stood to the side. "Come in. I understand you're staying at the inn for a few weeks. What has brought you here to Haven?"

"A forced vacation."

Bea's eyebrows rose. "Forced?"

"My parents, who fund a legal-aid office in Mobile, insisted I finally use my vacation days. It's their way of telling me I work too much."

"Why Haven?"

"Texas interests me, but I don't want to go to

a large city. I'm here for rest, not sightseeing. I thought I could help out while I was visiting. It's hard to go from working ten-hour days to no hours." When she'd been diagnosed six months ago with celiac disease, her parents were convinced the stress of her job had made her symptoms worse.

"She's met Nick and even helped with locating Corey last night," Carol said as Bea closed the front door.

The manager of the boys ranch grinned. "My, you've jumped right in. So you're familiar with ranches or, in your area, farms?"

"Well, no. But I'm a quick learner. I help out in my church's nursery as well as in a shelter for families. I love animals and children."

"Good. We have both," Bea said with a chuckle. "C'mon. I'll show you the house while Katie, our receptionist, calls down to the barn to have one of the other volunteers show you what we do there."

"I'd show you," Carol said with a chuckle, "but I'm a displaced city gal who can barely tell the difference between a cow and horse."

Bea laughed. "She isn't quite that bad, but I can attest to my friend being out of her element when she comes here."

"Give me another year, and I'll get the hang

of it. Darcy, you're young and probably not as set in your ways as I am."

As Bea escorted Darcy and Carol through the three different wings of the home that each housed up to eight residents, Darcy glimpsed the various ages of the children, often seeing older boys helping younger ones. In addition, she met some of the houseparents, their ages a wide span too. The home was large but had a warm, comfortable feel to it. She could see why Nick thought this place would be better for Corey than where he had been.

When Bea and Darcy returned to the director's office, she met Katie Ellis, who was talking with Nick. He swung his attention to Darcy as she entered the room.

"You have your car back already? What was wrong with it?" he asked in a Texan drawl.

"No, Carol brought me. Slim told me it was a glitch in the electrical system. Thanks for recommending him. He should have it done later this afternoon."

"He's the only one in town, but he's a good mechanic. Saves us having to go into Waco." Nick looked at Bea. "I finished taking care of trimming the horses' hooves. I can show Darcy the barn and some of the corrals before I need to leave. And Carol, I have to go into town. I can bring Darcy back to your place."

"I appreciate that. Clarence just texted me that he forgot to tell me about a dental appointment I have in half an hour and we have a new guest coming right after lunch." Carol glanced at Darcy. "You can go with me now or have the grand tour of the barn."

"I understand Corey is at the barn."

Nick nodded.

"I'd like to see how he's doing after last night and this morning at Mrs. Scott's."

Bea shook Darcy's hand. "Katie will give you the application to fill out, and we'll get the necessary information so you can start as soon as possible. We have all our volunteers do that. I hope to see you around even if your stay is temporary."

After Bea left, Katie gave Darcy a sheet of paper. "I'll take it after you fill it out. You won't regret volunteering here."

Darcy grinned. Based on what she had seen of the house, she had to agree with the receptionist. This would be perfect for her while she became acquainted with her biological father and made the decision whether to approach him or not. But, even more, she would have a chance to get to know Corey and possibly help him, even if he never knew she was his cousin.

And see Nick occasionally. The words sneaked into her mind and made her grin. She didn't understand why she responded to him. Maybe it was because he was so different from the men she knew at home.

Darcy turned to Nick, whose neutral expression told her nothing. "I'm ready. I'll fill out the form later."

As she walked in the direction of the barn, Nick pointed to her feet. "I'm glad you decided not to wear those heels you had on last night."

She chuckled. She'd probably looked as though she was going to her office rather than driving across country for eleven hours. Even working at Legal Aid, she always dressed as she would have if she'd worked for a big law firm. Her professionalism helped ease her clients' fear they wouldn't get good representation in court.

She slanted a look at Nick. "I still haven't gotten into vacation mode."

"How often do you take a vacation?"

"This will be my first in three years, since I finished law school. I'm not even sure I know how to slow down."

"Volunteering here won't necessarily be restful, but nothing beats helping these boys." He held the barn door open for her to enter first. "I'll introduce you to the ranch foreman. When I left, he was in the tack room showing Corey around."

A tall, rugged man stepped out of a room off to the right, accompanied by a black Lab. He smiled, deep creases at the sides of his blue eyes. "You must be the new volunteer Katie told me about. I'm Flint Rawlings."

News spread at sonic speed here. She shook his hand. "I'm Darcy Hill, and yes, I'm that person."

Corey came out of the tack room but hung back by the door.

"Do you want to help with the animals?" Flint asked Darcy.

When the black Lab sniffed her fingers, she petted him. "I love animals like dogs and cats, but I have to confess I haven't been around cattle, and the last time I was on a horse was several years ago." When her mare had died, she had walked away from riding. The memories of her horse robbed her of the pleasure she'd always gotten from riding. "But if you need help, I'm willing to learn."

"Flint, we could always use someone to clean out the stalls," Nick said next to her. "I can show her what to do." One corner of his mouth tilted up.

She got the impression Nick thought she didn't know how to get her hands dirty. She'd changed enough diapers while in the church nursery and cleaned Beauty's stall the ten years she had her. Their bond had gone beyond horse and rider. "Is it much different from cleaning out cages at an animal shelter? I used to volunteer there as a teenager." She decided she'd keep quiet about having her own horse.

Nick's face lit with a smile. "Not quite. On second thought, you'd fit in better at the house, maybe helping with homework or something like that."

"It's been nice to meet you, Darcy. I'm leaving to have lunch with Lana. She tutors the boys after school and has said on a few occasions they could always use more volunteers doing that."

"So what will it be? Mucking stalls or teaching kids?" Nick asked in a light tone.

But she also heard the challenge in Nick's voice. He thought she was a pampered socialite and couldn't do either task. Yes, she came from a wealthy family, but her father and mother always believed in working for what you wanted. As much as she would like to prove she was capable of mucking out a stall and doing much more with horses, she said to Flint, "I look forward to meeting Lana then. Tutoring the kids would be perfect for me." In that area she could help Corey, and that was the reason she'd come to the boys ranch.

"I'll tell her. C'mon, Cowboy." With his dog beside him, the ranch foreman left the barn.

"I think that's a wise choice," Nick murmured close to her ear, a dare still lingering. "Less messy."

She looked at Corey, his shoulders hunched, his head down. "What do you think, Corey? Mucking stalls or homework?"

The ten-year-old shrugged, his stare focused on the ground by his feet.

Nick walked to Corey and clasped his shoulder. "Let's give Darcy the grand tour."

The boy didn't reply but followed a step behind them. First Nick and then Darcy tried to include him, but they could only get one-word responses from him.

When Nick paused by the fence of one of the paddocks, he rested one booted foot on the bottom slat. "These are some of the horses the kids get to ride. They see to them. Several children are assigned to each horse and rotate duties every week."

Darcy paused next to Corey. "Which horse do you like the best?"

"Dunno," the boy mumbled.

"I think that's smart to check each one out before you commit to a horse." The urge to hug the child and tell him things would get better inundated her, but she wasn't even sure that was true. His dad could get Corey back and everything could remain the same as it had been before he was taken into state custody. She'd seen that happen working in her job.

Nick locked gazes with her for a brief moment and then shifted his attention to Corey. "C'mon, partner. I have to get you back to the house. Miss Bea still needs to show you the house."

As Nick settled behind the steering wheel and started his truck, he slanted a look at Darcy. "So what do you think about the boys ranch?"

"Corey is much better off here than with his dad. He's not happy right now, but then he wasn't happy at home."

"He's scared." That was why Bea had brought him to the barn first to see Nick. "In Dry Gulch, he had friends and knew some of the people, like Mrs. Scott. He'll feel better after he meets some of the other boys his age."

"What if he doesn't?"

"He's confused. He wants to be with his dad, and yet not if he's always being left alone. He doesn't know what to expect from day to day and certainly doesn't feel safe." Those same feelings used to plague Nick while he was growing up.

"I've dealt with kids like that."

"In a perfect world, Ned wouldn't drink and would love Corey unconditionally. But that isn't going to happen. Ned isn't going to change." He knew firsthand the mindset of an alcoholic and remembered the times his dad promised to stop drinking and reform. He never did; in fact he got worse.

"People can change. I've seen some turn their lives around."

Nick shook his head as he pulled away from the barn. "Ned is too far gone."

"How do you know that for sure?"

"I just do." He didn't share his past with anyone. It was a part of his life he wanted to wipe from his mind, but it was always there in the background. He never wanted to see a child grow up the way he had.

"Then I'll pray for the best for Corey."

"The best scenario would be the state taking Corey away from Ned and a family adopting him. I wish I was in a position to do it." The second he said that last sentence he wanted to snatch it back. He had no business being anyone's father.

"Because you're single? That might not matter in certain cases."

"I'm not dad material." How could he explain that he was struggling to erase the debt that his father had accumulated? If he lost the ranch, he would lose his home and job. But, more important, what if he wasn't a good father to Corey? It was one thing to be there to help when needed, but it was very different to be totally responsible for raising a child.

In the silence Darcy's stomach rumbled. She chuckled. "I guess I'm hungry. I've wanted to do something for you for helping me yesterday. I'd like to treat you to lunch."

"I don't—"

"You have to eat, and we don't have to take long. I know you said you had something to do in town. We could meet after that."

He'd been toying with the idea of talking to Fletcher again about Corey's situation, especially now that he had been moved to the boys ranch. Instead of paying Fletcher a visit at his office, Nick would eat lunch at Lila's Café, where the man often indulged in some of the best food in Haven.

"You're right. I do need to eat. I still have a long afternoon ahead at my ranch, but no work could keep me from being there for Corey when he arrived at his new home. When he gets scared, he clams up and sulks."

"Then he must have been really scared. He hardly said a word. I'm glad you were there for him. Do you think Ned will cause trouble for Corey?"

A vision of his own dad coming drunk to one of his baseball games and making a scene in the stands popped into his mind. Nick gripped the steering wheel so tightly his hands hurt. He had dropped the ball and the game had gone into extra innings. All he'd wanted to do was crawl into a hole and hide.

"Nick, are you okay?"

The concern in Darcy's voice pulled him away from the past, but the anger the memory produced lingered. "I'm fine."

"You're worried about Ned, but sometimes having a child taken away finally leads a parent to making the changes needed to reunite the family."

"And often it doesn't. And even if Ned stopped drinking in order to get Corey back, would it last? It's not easy to walk away from a habit that is so ingrained in you."

"But not impossible."

Nick pulled into a parking space near Lila's Café, switched off the engine and twisted toward her. "You want Ned to take Corey home." Anger laced each word.

She didn't flinch or turn away. Instead, she shifted to face him. "I want what's best for Corey. The same as you. The boys ranch is nice and a good temporary situation for Corey, but it isn't a home with a family."

"You grew up with a mother and father always there for you?"

She nodded. "Family is everything."

"That's nice and I agree—when it's available. But this isn't a perfect world where all children grow up with a loving family."

"You don't think I know that? I work with dysfunctional families all the time in my job. But we can't give up on the family. That's the fabric of our society. When the family goes, everyone is hurt."

She was right about the importance of family, but she looked at life through rose-colored glasses. "Are you one of those do-gooders who thinks all you have to do is throw a little money at a problem or breeze in and out of a person's life and it will change?"

Her blue eyes narrowed to diamond-hard chips. "You don't know me or what I've been through. I'm sorry you didn't have a family—"

"Hold it right there. Who said I didn't?"

"You did. If you had, you wouldn't feel the way you do."

The truth in her words deflated his anger. This whole affair with Ned had brought back painful memories he had tried to forget. "You're right. I didn't have the perfect family with loving parents. My father was just like Ned and my mother died when I was seven."

"I'm sorry."

"I didn't tell you to get your sympathy. I've dealt with it and moved on."

"Have you?"

He looked long and hard into her eyes. "Yes. My dad died eighteen months back, and the world is a better place now. Nothing else I can do about it."

"Yes, there is. You can forgive him."

He glared at her. Forgive his father? No way! "If you're hungry, I suggest we go inside. I've worked up quite an appetite."

"For what, rattlesnake meat?"

He paused in opening the truck door and glanced over his shoulder at the twinkle in her eye.

"I couldn't resist saying that," Darcy said with a smile and climbed down from the pickup.

How in the world did the conversation end up on subjects he never talked to others about—even his uncle? What was so different about Darcy that he let himself be baited? He shook off the feelings she'd stirred about his past and smiled back. "If you want, we could go rattlesnake hunting while you're here. I know people who do."

"I'll pass on that."

He winked. "You have an open invitation if you change your mind."

She laughed. At the entrance to the café, Nick opened the door for her. As he entered behind her, he spied one empty table in the back corner, not far from where Fletcher was eating with the mayor, Elsa Wells. No doubt Fletcher was trying to sway her to his way of thinking about the boys ranch.

While passing their table, Nick slowed and tipped the brim of his cowboy hat toward Elsa before stopping next to Fletcher and staring down at him. "I thought you should know, since you're related to Corey Phillips, he's now residing at the boys ranch—in case you want to visit your cousin there." He couldn't resist that last dig.

Then Nick continued toward the vacant table and held the chair out for Darcy. As she settled, he took his seat across from her, facing Fletcher. The older man's gaze stabbed through him.

"Who was that?"

"That's Fletcher Phillips and Elsa Wells, our mayor."

"I saw him this morning picking up Avery Culpepper. She's staying at the Blue Bonnet Inn."

After the waitress filled their glasses with water and handed them a menu, he opened it, saying, "What do you think about Avery?"

"She's a bit young for Fletcher."

He stared at her for a few seconds and then laughed. "She's made it clear she isn't happy that her grandfather left his place to the boys ranch. She has said that she won't hire a lawyer and take the Lone Star Cowboy League and the boys ranch to court if she receives a hundred thousand dollars. The league turned her down."

"So has she hired Fletcher Phillips to represent her?"

"Not sure, although they have been chummy."

Darcy studied her menu and then lifted her head. "Is the lawyer the reason we came to eat here?"

"I was going to pay him another visit at his office, but you're right that I do have to eat, so why not do both at the same time?"

"I like the way you think. What are you getting for lunch?"

"Chicken-fried steak. They make the best in the county."

"With mashed potatoes and gravy?"

He nodded.

"Sounds delicious, but I'm on a gluten-free diet. I have to be careful what I eat. I'll order a salad instead."

Surprise flitted through him, and yet it shouldn't have. Darcy was thin and probably constantly watching what she ate and dieting. She seemed so out of place here.

So many things about Darcy just didn't seem to add up. Her desire to help with the search for Corey and to volunteer at the boys ranch was astonishing for someone who was here on vacation. There was something else going on here. He felt it in his gut. Just what was Darcy's real story?

Chapter Five

The following Monday afternoon, Darcy entered the library at the boys ranch and scanned the room for Lana Alvarez. She spied the school teacher/volunteer at a table with two boys.

As Darcy approached, Lana lifted her head and smiled, her dark brown eyes fixed on Darcy.

"I'm Darcy Hill. I'm hoping I can help you with tutoring." She held out her hand.

Lana shook it. "We always need extra tutors." Lana rose and moved away from the boys. "Flint told me you helped Nick find Corey."

"Yes, and I was hoping I could work with him especially. I want to help him adjust to his new situation." Darcy searched the library for Corey and found him at a table alone.

"That can certainly be arranged. This is all so new. I think he feels a bit overwhelmed."

"I agree. He's staring at that book, but I don't think he's reading."

"Today was his first day at school. I don't know a lot about him yet. I was going to finish with Danny and Mikey, and then see what he needs to do."

Darcy looked around the room. "I can see why you need help. There are only a few volunteers."

"It varies from day to day. I hear you'll only be here for the rest of this month."

"Right, but while I'm in Haven, I can be here every day to help out." Seeing Corey sitting by himself bothered Darcy. "I hate to see him alone."

"Aiden asked him to sit with him, but Corey didn't want to. Aiden hasn't been here long, and he lives in the same wing as Corey. I think he'll be good for Corey."

"Which one is Aiden?"

"The table to the left, brown hair. If you can help Corey, that would be great. Sometimes it takes a new boy a little time to fit in, but Corey isn't even trying."

"Thanks. I'll see what I can do."

Darcy made her way to Corey and took the chair next to the boy. He stiffened, but he slid a glance her way. "How was the first day of school?" she asked him.

He shrugged.

"Did you meet any friends?"

He shook his head.

"Have you seen Nick today?"

He nodded.

Darcy touched the corner of his book titled *The Adventures of Shaun*. "This isn't a textbook. Did you get it at school?"

His head bobbed up and down.

She'd dealt before with children who occasionally would give her the silent treatment. She decided to ask him a question he couldn't answer with a yes or no. "Who's your new teacher?"

He didn't say anything for a long moment and then murmured, "Mrs. Harris."

"What are some of the things you did today at school?"

"Work."

"What do you have to do for homework? Math? Reading?"

"A report on the library book that I checked out."

Darcy peered at the page he was on. He'd read only two pages. "You haven't read much. When is the report due?"

"End of the week."

"Why did you pick it?"

"It was the last one left on the book cart for the class."

She picked it up and read the back-cover copy.

"This sounds really interesting. Shaun and his friends find a secret cave with a treasure in it. I'd love for you to read some of it to me."

His head dropped and his shoulders hunched.

"This isn't the best place to read a story. Let's go into the house and find a quiet area."

He mumbled something she couldn't hear.

Darcy leaned closer. "What did you say?"

He slammed the book closed and leaped to his feet. Darcy stood and grabbed *The Adventures of Shaun* while Corey hurried from the library.

As she passed Lana, she said, "I've got this." She prayed she did.

Then Darcy rushed across the short distance to the house. Walking down a hallway, she looked right and left. Which way did Corey go?

Darcy checked the living room but didn't find Corey. When she left, she glimpsed him sitting on a step near the top of the staircase. Corey tensed and then started to stand.

She slowly ascended the stairs. "Relax, Corey. You don't have to read if you don't want to."

Corey's eyes widened as though he felt trapped.

"I'm only here to help you." She sat beside him. "Coming to a new place can be scary. I remember the first time I went to summer camp. I was eight and didn't know anyone. A lot of kids knew each other from the summer before. The first day I hid a lot. I had such a good hiding place that I didn't realize the whole camp was looking for me. I missed dinner."

"Where did you hide?"

"Under the porch."

"What about the bugs and critters?"

"I was fine until a snake slithered in front of me. I got out of there so fast, I fell and rolled down the hill. I landed at my counselor's feet."

Corey giggled. "Was she mad at you?"

"She wasn't happy, but the other campers couldn't believe I crawled under there and stayed. Now, I don't recommend doing this, but after that, I had a lot of kids who wanted to talk to me."

"I don't mind snakes."

"I never thought about it until I encountered one under the porch, but now they're one of my least favorite animals. I have several pets at home. My parents are watching them while I'm here."

Corey twisted toward her. "I've never had a pet. What kind do you have?"

"A cat named Calico and a dog named Arnold."

"They get along?"

"Best buddies."

"Do you miss them?"

"Yup. If you could have a pet, what would you get?"

"A dog. I liked meeting Cowboy at the barn."

"How about the horses?"

"Yes!"

Maybe Nick would be at the barn. "Well, then, let's go to the barn. I'll let Lana know we're going for a walk."

"But I'm supposed to do my homework."

"You will afterward."

He turned forward and lowered his head. "I can't."

"I'll help you."

"You don't understand. I can't read real good."

His behavior made sense. Did the school and boys ranch know he had a problem? "Tell you what. Let's go find a quiet spot and I'll read the first page if you'll try the second one. That's all for today. Then we can both go to the barn and see the animals for the rest of the time."

"Only a page?"

She nodded.

Corey jumped to his feet and hurried down the stairs. More slowly, Darcy followed. She'd just found something that might motivate the boy. She couldn't wait to tell Nick.

As the sun set, Nick brushed down Laredo after riding him along the perimeter of his ranch to check the fences. He did that more frequently since the one along his northern boundary had been sabotaged. Finally they all appeared to be in good condition. His dad must not have fixed any in years. That went for a lot of things around the place, but after sixteen months of hard work he was beginning to see daylight.

The barn door opened behind him. Weary from a long day that had started at five in the morning, he looked over his shoulder, brushed his gelding's flank one last time and then rotated toward Darcy. The sight of her lifted his spirits. "What brings you to the Flying Eagle?"

Her smile lit the dimness in the cavernous barn. "I came to see you. Your uncle told me you were here."

He held the halter and led Laredo in the direction of the back door. "I'm gonna put him out to pasture and then I'll be right back."

Why was she here? Over the weekend he'd hoped she would be at the boys ranch when he was there. Lana had told him she'd dropped by after church yesterday to set up times for her to volunteer, but he'd arrived in the late afternoon and missed her. He'd felt disappointed and knew he needed to stop thinking about her. Easy to say, hard to do. There was something captivating about her—fragile and yet not.

After reentering the barn, he crossed to the tack room and hung up the halter. He knew the exact second she stood in the doorway, although she didn't make a sound. Her presence was almost tangible.

Slowly he faced her. Her shoulder-length blond hair framed her beautiful features. Her bluc gaze held his for a long moment. As he crossed to her, breathing in her flowery scent, which chased away the smells of the barn, his look dropped to her full lips. They were covered in a light pink gloss. He balled his hand to suppress the urge to touch them. *To kiss them.*

A whinny destroyed the moment. Darcy stepped back, and he skirted around her, needing to put some space between them. If he was smart, he would remember to keep his distance, but clear across the town wasn't far enough to stop him from wanting to cup her face and…

He refused to complete the thought. "So why are you here?" Nick asked as he strolled toward a stall containing a pregnant mare. Before he left he wanted to check on her.

"I came to talk about Corey."

He opened the door and went insidc to assess Morning Star, running his hand over her. "I took Bea and him to school this morning. I'd promised him I would for his first day. He was quiet, but he seemed all right. One of the boys on his wing is in the same class—Aiden. When I left just before the bell rang, they were talking together."

"That's good. But he was sullen when he came home."

Nick gave Morning Star a carrot. "It won't be long, girl. I'll see you before I go to bed." After rubbing her nose, he left the stall, closing the door.

"She looks pregnant. Is that why she's in the barn? Most of the stalls are empty."

"Yes. The first foal she had last year died not long after she gave birth. I want to keep an eye on her this time."

"That would be something Corey would get a kick out of."

"You've been with him a few days, and you think you know him."

"Today he told me he never had a pet but would love a dog. When we went to the barn, he said he wanted to learn to ride. Horses were his second favorite animal."

How had she discovered so much about Corey in such a short time? He didn't know about the child wanting a dog. Things like this only confirmed to Nick that he wasn't father material. "I promised him I would teach him to ride, but then Ned wouldn't let me bring him to my ranch."

"Flint told Corey he would be put in a group to care for one of the horses. He smiled all the way back to the house."

Nick gestured toward a hay bale. "Have a seat."

"I probably shouldn't stay long."

As she sat, he leaned one shoulder against the wall of the barn. "How did you find me?"

"Bea told me where you live. Just down the road from the boys ranch."

"Yes, it's convenient for me to pop over there when I can, even for half an hour or so. How did it go with Corey today? Lana told me you were volunteering to help with homework after school." And he'd purposely stayed away. He needed to get her out of his head.

"Today there were only four of us for twenty-four kids. Thankfully the younger ones didn't have that much homework. Corey took up my whole time."

"Why?"

"He wouldn't do his work. Just sat there staring at the page. He finally told me he has trouble reading. The book he had to read was too hard for him."

"I've helped him with math, but he never asked for any help with reading. He's good at math and really didn't need much assistance." Nick sank onto the hay bale next to Darcy. Yet another thing Darcy had discovered about Corey that he hadn't known.

"He didn't admit it easily, but at least now I know how to work with him. I let Lana know. She'll talk with his teacher tomorrow."

"How was his reading?"

"Slow. He retained what he read, but he struggled with quite a few words that someone his age should know. I told him I would make flash cards of the ones he had trouble with and we'd review them."

"It sounds like you'll be spending most of your time with Corey."

She grinned. "I enjoyed this afternoon. Lana and I decided I would work primarily with Corey. Tomorrow there will be more volunteers. Monday seems to have the least number of people. Maybe you could help out with the homework."

"Me?" He pointed at his chest. "I think I'll stick with helping in other ways. The extent of my higher education was one year at a junior college before I joined the army. The only teaching I'm gonna do is how to ride a horse." Another thing they didn't have in common. She'd gone to law school after four years of college. They were so different, and he needed to remember that. He stood and held out his hand for her. "I appreciate you letting me know."

She allowed him to help her to her feet, which brought her within inches of him. Again her light, sweet scent teased his senses. "I'd love to be there when you give him his first riding lesson. I hope you'll let me know. I have a lot of spare time on my hands."

"And that bothers you?"

"*Bother* isn't quite the word I would pick. I'm used to being busy. By the time I adjust to this leisure, my vacation will be over."

"Uncle Howard is preparing stew tonight. He makes it from scratch with tons of vegetables and beef and always fixes a big pot of it. Why don't you join us before you head back to the inn? That is, unless you have something else to do."

Her smile encompassed her whole face. "I got a whiff of it when I was up at your house. It smelled great. So yes, I'd love to."

He automatically reacted to her grin with one of his own. The weariness he'd felt earlier vanished as though her presence charged his energy. "Good. Let's go. I'm starving. Forgot to eat lunch."

"I didn't, and I'm still starving."

Nick shut the barn door behind him as they left. "You might like the temperature for the rest of the week. It'll be in the sixties."

"Now, that's getting closer to what I'm used to in January."

"Did Corey say much about his first day at school?"

"Not much except that his teacher was nice."

"I hope this works for him. Did he mention his dad?"

"No. We mostly talked about the animals. Why?"

Nick paused on the back-door stoop. "Because I got a call from Mrs. Scott this morning. Since Ned was released on bail, he hasn't left his house. He came home not long after Corey was taken to the ranch, went inside and stayed."

"Do you think something is wrong?"

He let her go into the house first. "I imagine he's holed up, drinking. I asked Mrs. Scott to go check on him and to call me. She tried, but no one answered the door."

"Are you going to visit him?"

"I might." He felt he owed Corey that, but being around Ned always left Nick stuck in the past.

"I can go with you. I don't think you should go alone."

"Go alone where?" Uncle Howard entered the kitchen.

"To see if Corey's dad is all right." Nick strolled across the room. "I need to wash up. I'll be back in ten minutes or so. Ask my uncle if he's used anything with gluten in the stew."

Nick headed for a quick shower after a hard day of labor. He didn't want her to think he was making a big deal that she was here sharing dinner with him.

He rubbed the steam off the mirror and stared at himself, his beard a day old. He hadn't shaved this morning because he was running late to take Corey to school.

What are you doing? She'll be gone from Haven at the end of the month, if she even stays that long.

Five minutes later, he hastened back to the kitchen, the sound of laughter drifting to him.

Uncle Howard raised both eyebrows when Nick entered. He sent his uncle a narrowed look that he hoped conveyed Howard better not say a word about his showering and cleaning up.

"So what's so funny?" Nick approached the table, not sure where to sit, across from Darcy or catty-cornered.

"Howard was telling me about when you came to visit him in Galveston."

"About the time I sneaked up into the attic and fell partway through the ceiling?"

"Yes. I can just picture you swinging your legs around, trying not to fall all the way through." Darcy took a sip of her iced tea.

Her teasing look mesmerized him for a few seconds. "I was trying to pull myself up through the hole before Uncle Howard found out what I'd done."

"You didn't think the hole in the ceiling would clue him in?"

"I was eight. I wasn't thinking that far ahead." He didn't tell her he'd been in the attic hiding so he didn't have to return to Haven later that day.

Darcy chuckled. "I don't want you to ever talk to my parents. My curiosity got me into a lot of trouble. But I have to admit they took it in stride."

Whereas his dad hadn't. At least his problems with his father helped him to relate to Corey. "Now you've stirred my curiosity. What kind of trouble?"

A twinkle danced in her blue eyes, brightening the sparkle in them. "I used to open all my Christmas gifts and then seal them back up so my parents didn't know. I couldn't stand the waiting. They got wise to me and didn't put anything out until after I went to bed Christmas Eve."

He'd rarely received a present from his dad, but this topic was bringing back too many memories he was determined not to remember. Ever since he'd begun watching out for Corey, he'd relived his past over and over, and now his conversation with Darcy was having the same effect.

"What time will you be finished working with Corey tomorrow? I want him to choose his horse and start learning how to take care of it," Nick said, changing the subject.

"If Corey has his way, as soon as he comes back to the boys ranch after school. I can bring him to the barn after he completes his homework. He usually doesn't have much."

"I think I'll hitch a ride with you, Nick. I haven't seen Corey since Ned stop letting him come to our ranch." Uncle Howard bowed his head. "Let's say grace and eat this beef stew before it gets cold."

After grace, his uncle started passing the food. "Darcy, how in the world did you end up here in Haven? Did you throw a dart at the map of Texas?"

"The name was what sold me on this town. I had a difficult case right before I came here. A custody battle between a husband and wife with two children caught in the middle. The two had a tug of war with the children."

"Did it end okay?" Nick wasn't surprised the parents were using their children as pawns.

"Yes, because the judge was firm but patient. He came up with a decision that made the two parents agree to a friendlier solution."

Uncle Howard broke a piece of bread and dunked part of it into his stew. "Something like Solomon when the two women claimed the same child?"

"Yes, neither parent wanted to give up seeing one of their children. They both were fighting for full-time custody. The hate in the courtroom was palpable. Each night when I left them, it was hard to decompress. I needed a break, and my boss insisted I take it."

Those poor children would have to deal with each parent's hostility against the other. What he'd seen of families only reinforced he didn't want to have kids. "Do you work with families a lot?" Nick dipped his spoon into the beef stew.

"At least a third of my clients. But enough about me. What do y'all do on the ranch? I've seen some horses and a pasture full of cattle." Darcy shifted her gaze between Nick and his uncle.

"The Flying Eagle has two thousand acres, considered small compared to other Texan cattle ranches. We have one hundred and twenty head of cattle and about ten horses. I'd love to acquire more horses to train, but with a staff of only myself, Uncle Howard and hired hands during the busy times, that's not possible." One day Nick hoped he could. Cattle were his business, but his interest and love were horses.

As his uncle expounded on some of the everyday duties, Nick watched Darcy focus her total attention on him. She seemed genuinely interested in the ranch, and yet, even dressed in her more casual clothes, she had *expensive taste* stamped all over her, from her Ray-Ban sunglasses to her Louis Vuitton purse.

When dinner was over, Uncle Howard waved them out of the kitchen. "You're a guest. I can handle the dinner dishes."

In the hallway that led to the front of the house, Darcy sighed. "His beef stew was delicious. And the bread smelled so wonderful that my mouth watered, but I can't eat bread made with wheat."

With his gaze fixed on the aforementioned mouth, Nick grappled for something to say. Between the exhaustion creeping through his body and his losing battle to keep himself from staring at her, his mind went blank.

"Are you okay?" Darcy asked in the entry hall.

Yeah, as soon as you leave. "I'm fine. I'm just tired from riding around those two thousand acres checking fences, cattle and the land itself."

"At least the snow melted and the temperature was above freezing." At the front door, she turned toward him, not a foot away.

All the reasons he should stay away from her raced through his mind, but all he wanted to think about was how it would feel to kiss her. She was the breath of fresh air he'd needed ever since coming home to Haven last year.

He reached around her, brushing against her

arm, and grasped the door handle. "Good night. I'll see you tomorrow after Corey finishes his homework." He opened the door and quickly put some room between them.

She smiled at him, her crystalline blue eyes enticing him to come closer. To taste her lips.

He stepped back. "Bye."

Then, he remained in the doorway watching her—until her taillights vanished in the dark.

He had to stay away from her. She was here temporarily and they had nothing in common. End of story.

But one word seeped into his thoughts: *Corey.*

Chapter Six

"That's correct, Corey." Darcy sat next to the ten-year-old as he finished his reading home work in the living room the next afternoon.

He slammed the book closed and hopped up, grabbing his school backpack. "Let's go. It's time to meet Nick. Aiden is comin' when he gets through his homework."

Corey had worked twice as hard as he had the day before. She needed him to have an incentive every afternoon. Maybe she could talk Nick into coming to work this time every day. She smiled at the thought. She would get to see Nick as well as Corey. She liked that plan.

Corey stopped at the living room entrance and looked back at her. "C'mon. I don't wanna be late."

"What do we do with your books?"

"In here." He took them from her and stuffed

them in his backpack, then he started for the front door.

"Corey, you need to put on your jacket."

"Oh, yeah. Forgot." After shrugging into his coat, he added. "Now can we go?"

"Yes."

He shot outside so fast she'd have to jog to keep up with him. Corey's attitude today had improved so much. One reason was the lesson with Nick, but also today Aiden and Corey had played at recess.

She allowed him to race ahead of her. The chill in the wind cut through her. She was used to a breeze from the Gulf, but this wasn't like that. She began to wonder if it would snow again.

She'd been looking forward to seeing Nick herself, but she didn't want to seem too eager. She liked that they were different. She'd dated plenty of men who were from a similar background and career, but no one had stayed in her thoughts as much as Nick did. She wanted to attribute it to their mutual interest in Corey. But that wasn't it. Nick kept himself closed off from others. Last night with his uncle was the first time she'd seen him really relax, especially as they talked about the Flying Eagle.

When she entered the barn, Corey had already left his backpack near the tack room and was hurrying toward Nick at the far end. Nick smiled when he spied the boy. Then he scanned the area, and his gaze latched onto her. Her heartbeat sped as she approached the pair, Nick's eyes still locked with hers as though she was roped and he was drawing her to him.

"Corey said he got all his homework done."

She nodded. "He really buckled down and did a great job."

Corey beamed. "I already know which horse I want. Ginger. Aiden said they needed another person on his team."

"Sounds good to me," Nick said. "You'll make the third one in Aiden and Ben Turner's group."

Corey's forehead creased. "I've seen him but haven't talked to him. He's in wing one."

"Each team has at least one older boy. Let's go get Ginger in the paddock and bring her in here. I'm going to teach you how to saddle her."

"When do I get to ride her?"

"When you know how to care for her and can do every step that leads up to riding her."

"I'll stay back while y'all get Ginger." Darcy stood at the back door as they left. Sheltered by the barn, she watched them enter a corral, a halter in Nick's hand. Corey seemed to listen intently to every word Nick said.

So did Darcy. His slow Texan drawl reminded her of warm butter dripping from a freshly baked biscuit. Forbidden to her.

As Nick showed Corey what to do, a loud voice boomed through the cavernous barn. "Where's…my son?"

Darcy turned toward the man who was slurring his words as though he'd been drinking. At the other end of the barn stood Ned Phillips, his face set in anger. She looked around for anyone else in the barn. No one was there but her and her cousin.

Ned stormed toward Darcy, pointing at her. "I've seen you. Where's Corey? I'm bringing him home. Ain't no one taking my son away from me."

Darcy shut the door behind her and braced herself in front of it. "He's not here, as you can see. You need to leave."

Ned cursed. "I saw him come in here. He's hidin' again. Corey, come out here. Now!" He shouted the last word so loudly that his voice rang through her head. She hoped Nick had heard and would keep the child away.

Instead, the back door banged open, and Nick filled the entrance with his large presence. His arms stiff at his side, he curled and uncurled his hands. "You don't belong here. You need to leave. Now." His emphasis on the same word Ned had used was so different—it was quietly spoken with a commanding tone.

Ned cut the distance between him and Nick. "And you do?"

"I help take care of the horses." Nick's voice dropped even quieter.

Ned thrust his face even closer to Nick's. "Where is *my* son?"

"You reek of alcohol. Someone will drive you home. Then, if you want to see Corey, call the boys ranch office to find out the procedure."

"What? He's mine, not yours."

"He's not a piece of property."

Ned whirled around and stumbled forward. He headed for the stall nearest him. "Corey?" Then he searched the next one.

Darcy moved quickly to Nick and whispered, "I'll take Corey up to the house and let them know what's happening down here."

"He's right out back, holding the reins to Ginger. Tie the mare to the fence and go. I'll keep Ned in here while you do."

"But—"

He bent forward and murmured into her ear, "Go."

She hurried out the back as she heard a stall door slamming closed. "Let's go to the house."

Fear seemed to freeze the child against the barn, his eyes huge.

Darcy stepped to his side and took his free hand. "I'll be with you the whole way."

"But—but Dad's..." He choked on his tears. "I don't want to go home."

"You aren't going to." All she wanted to do was hold him and keep him safe. "Come on." With her arm around Corey's shoulder, she guided him to the nearest fence and helped his trembling fingers tie the reins.

"Get out of my way," Ned yelled from inside the barn.

Darcy grabbed Corey's hand and started for the house. Her cousin kept glancing over his shoulder.

She caught his attention. "I'm not going to let anything happen to you, Corey. Neither is Nick."

He looked up at her, tears filling his eyes. "He must be drinkin'. He usually yells like that when he is."

As they mounted the steps to the porch, the door swung open and a boy about Corey's age with brown hair and eyes came outside. "I was just coming to the barn. What happened?"

"Let's all go inside. Can you go find Miss Bea?" she asked the other kid.

He nodded and raced toward the back of the house.

"That's my new friend, Aiden." Corey's face reddened. "I don't want him to see my dad drunk."

"He won't." She guided him to the living room

couch. It was in front of the window that looked out onto the porch. "We'll wait here for Miss Bea." After settling, Darcy put her arm around Corey and drew him close.

Corey's trembling body stirred maternal instincts in Darcy to protect this child at any cost. He stared down, eyes glued to his lap. Even when Bea hastened into the room, he didn't look up but only curled closer to Darcy.

"Aiden told me you needed to see me."

"Where's Aiden?"

"He's worried about Corey. I told him to go to his wing and let one of their houseparents know I need to see them." She closed the distance between them and sat on the other side of Corey.

"His dad showed up in the barn. I think he'd been watching. He'd seen Corey going in." Darcy lowered her voice. "He was drunk. Nick's taking care of him."

Bea withdrew her cell phone from her pocket and placed a call. "Flint, I need you to go to the barn. Corey's dad is there. He's been drinking."

When the boys ranch's director disconnected the call, Corey yanked his head up and said, sobbing, "He isn't a bad man. Only when he's drinking." Then he buried his face against Darcy.

No child should have to deal with that.

Darcy wrapped her arms about him, sheltering him the only way she could.

Standing in front of the barn door, Nick held his palm out. "Ned, I'm driving you home. Give me your keys," he said in a commanding voice.

Red-faced, Ned glared at him. "You have no right to keep me from Corey." He stepped back and swayed.

"If you want to see him, I told you to go through the proper channels."

"I—I dunno..." Ned latched on to a post nearby. "I need a drink."

"No." Nick prepared himself for a fight as he came toward the man with bloodshot eyes, who was frantically looking around. "Give me your car keys. You're going home."

"You can't—" Ned paused, blinking rapidly "—make me."

The barn door behind Ned flew open, and Flint rushed inside. Nick was relieved to have help. He'd seen Ned go off, much like his dad used to.

Ned peered at Nick, his arms falling from the post. His hands fisted. He took one step toward Nick, rocked from side to side and then collapsed to the ground.

As Nick knelt by Ned and checked for a pulse, Flint hurried to them. "Is he alive?"

"Yes. Just passed out, which will make getting him into his car a little easier."

"Thank the Lord. It looked like he was going after you." Flint squatted near Ned's legs. "I saw an old Chevy outside next to your truck. Is that his car?"

"Yep." Nick patted Ned's pockets until he found the keys. "I'm gonna drive him back to his house. Can you follow me and bring me back here for my truck?"

"I wish I could. I have to attend a parents' meeting about the baseball league. I'm going to coach Logan's team. I could try to get out—"

"No, don't. I'll see if Darcy is available. I didn't get the impression that she had plans this evening." For a second Nick was surprised that the person he'd thought of immediately was Darcy—not his uncle or someone else at the boys ranch.

Flint gripped Ned's legs, while Nick took his arms. The smell of alcohol was nauseating. "Are you sure?"

"I can always get Uncle Howard to help if Darcy can't. Ned might not be my friend, but I can't let him stay here and sleep it off or drive somewhere else."

"You could call the sheriff to deal with the man."

A blast of cold air blew through the barn's

front entrance as Nick maneuvered through it. "He's in enough trouble with the sheriff after what he did last week with Corey. Let's put him in his backseat."

Flint dropped Ned's legs and opened the car door. "Did Corey see his dad?"

"No. I had him stay outside with Ginger." After Nick and Flint wrestled to get Ned inside the Chevy, Nick climbed into the front. "Thanks for the help. I'll drive up to the house and see if Darcy can follow me."

"There's always the sheriff," Flint said and jogged toward his place on the ranch.

Even if Darcy couldn't drive to Dry Gulch, Nick wanted to stop by the main house to see how Corey was feeling about his father being at the boys ranch.

He left Ned sleeping his drunken stupor off in the back of the beat-up Chevy while Nick climbed the steps to the porch. The door opened before he could ring the bell.

His gaze fixed onto Darcy's concerned face. "How's Corey?"

"He went to his wing with his friend a couple of minutes ago. Where's Ned?"

Nick jerked his thumb toward the car parked next to Darcy's Corvette. "In the backseat, passed out. I'm driving him home. Could you follow me and bring me back here for my truck?"

"Sure. Let me get my coat and tell Bea I'm leaving."

Nick returned to the Chevy to make sure Ned was still asleep. He waited to get into Ned's car until Darcy appeared a few minutes later and got into hers. He pulled away from the house, contemplating rolling down his window. The stench of alcohol brought back memories of taking care of his father after he would finally pass out, much to his relief. Now, Nick's stomach roiled.

The thirty-minute drive was thirty minutes longer than Nick wanted. Visions of his dad yelling like Ned just had paraded across his mind.

When Nick drove into Ned's driveway, all he wanted to do was get him inside and leave. As he climbed out and drew in a deep breath of fresh air, Darcy parked behind him.

Approaching him, she asked, "Do you need help getting him out of the car?"

"I can manage. It's not far to his house. If you can unlock the door and hold it open, I'll get him inside." He gave her the set of keys. "I don't know which one fits the lock."

While Darcy began working on opening the front door, Nick put his arms under Ned's armpits and pulled him from the back. Then, clasping Ned's upper body, Nick dragged him into the house and, with Darcy's help, laid him on the couch.

She picked up a blanket from the floor and covered Ned with it. Then she backed away and scanned the living room. "Was the place this bad when Corey was here?"

"Yes." He swept his gaze over the piles of clothes on the floor, the half-eaten food sitting on the table and two almost-empty bottles of liquor.

He grabbed them, headed for the kitchen and poured the alcohol down the drain. Then he tossed them into the overflowing trash can.

"Wow. What died in here?" Darcy asked from the doorway.

"Probably more than one thing. Let's get out of here before this smell is permanently ingrained into my mind."

She held up the keys on a chain. "What do you want to do with these?"

"Hide them. Then he can call me to find out where they are." Nick took them from Darcy, strode to the couch and stuck them under a cushion Ned slept on.

A few minutes later, settled in Darcy's Corvette, Nick finally relaxed his tensed muscles. "I hope that's the last time I have to do that, but

I wouldn't be surprised if he showed up at the boys ranch again."

"Unless something drastic happens, I doubt Corey's dad will change. In my job I've dealt with alcoholics on more occasions than I liked. They said they wanted help, but I never had but one follow through with what I arranged for them."

"They have to hit rock bottom before it really has a chance to work, and even then it's a hard road." Nick's father never did reach this point. He lived in denial his whole life.

He took out his cell phone. "Maybe you really don't believe that as much as you think." Then he called his uncle and told him the reason he was running late was Ned's unexpected visit to the boys ranch. He needed to check on Corey.

"I can save dinner," Howard said. "I just started. I was with Morning Star. I think she'll have her foal tonight. I'm going back and forth to the barn."

Probably, which meant a long night for him. "She's due."

"If Darcy wants to come to eat with us again, I have more than enough for her."

What was his uncle up to? He would have to talk to Uncle Howard about the fact that Darcy was only in town temporarily and had a good life in Alabama. "We'll see." Nick hung up.

"How's your uncle doing?" Darcy asked.

"Fine. He thinks Morning Star will deliver tonight."

"Really? How exciting. When I was a child, I was there when my dog had puppies and for a few days I dreamed of being a veterinarian. But Dad was a lawyer, so I went that route. You probably understand with your family ranch."

Love for the Flying Eagle was one thing his father hadn't managed to destroy—at least he hoped so. "I wanted to be a cowboy ever since I can remember." At first he'd been trying to please his dad, but later it became about much more. He was going to prove he could make it alone. "My roots are deep here. When I served in the army, I longed for Haven."

"I love where I grew up. That's how I feel." She slid a glance toward him and then turned into the boys ranch.

He knew she did volunteer work in Alabama, but why had she become attached to Corey so quickly? Her first encounter with the boy was when he ran away from home. Maybe it was because she was used to dealing with people in trouble in her job. She had a big heart.

"See, we have something in common. I knew we would."

"Why?"

"Because we both care for Corey. Before you

called your uncle, you said something about how I really don't think people can change. I think they can or I would have given up on the one person I dealt with who was an alcoholic and did become sober. Still is."

"Who?"

"My college roommate." Darcy pulled up to the main house and parked. "You said something to your uncle about checking on Corey before you went home. I'd also like to. I'm hoping he won't be so distressed now since we made sure his father got home okay."

"Sure. I'm glad you are. He's feeling pretty alone right now. I know Bea and the staff will do what they can, but no matter how upset he was before he came to the ranch, his home in Dry Gulch was familiar to him, at least." In his childhood, Nick had clung to that fact. He'd disappear for hours on the ranch when his dad was angry or drinking.

"You think Corey should have stayed with his dad?"

"No, but his emotions will be all over the place. However, the staff at the boys ranch has dealt with that before. And the place can give him one of the things he needs—to feel safe."

"That can really help him adjust more quickly. His close relationship with you will help too. You're good with him."

"Thanks," he mumbled, the compliment taking him by surprise. Her words touched a part of his heart he'd kept from others for years. He'd always wanted to make a difference in someone's life and had thought being a soldier was the answer. Instead, all the death and destruction had isolated him even more.

They both exited the Corvette and headed to the front entrance. Lana answered the door and let them inside.

"I was just about to leave. I'm glad I waited. How is Corey's dad? Flint told me he helped you get the man into his car."

"We left him on his couch sleeping it off." Nick took his cowboy hat off and hung it on a peg.

"Good, because Corey has been asking about him."

"We wanted to check on him. Where is he?" Darcy asked.

"In the rec room with some of the boys. There's a ping-pong tournament going on."

"Thanks, Lana. See you tomorrow for study hall."

Nick led the way to the rec room, a large open space with tables and chairs. Boys crowded at one end where two were playing ping-pong. He searched for Corey and found him leaning against the wall, not really paying attention to the game.

"It'll be hard to talk privately with him in here. Do you know where we could go with Corey? I noticed when we passed the living room there were several groups in there." Darcy walked with Nick toward Corey.

"There's a small room near Bea's office. She uses it for counseling and as a place where parents can meet with their child."

As they approached Corey, he stared at a spot on the floor between him and the group of boys. Nick remembered often retreating—if not physically, at least emotionally—from what was going on around him.

He cleared his throat and gave Corey time to look up at him. "Let's go talk."

Corey didn't say anything until he'd left the rec room. In the hallway, he asked, "How's Dad?"

"He's home safe and sleeping." Nick clasped his shoulder.

"It's all my fault."

Nick waited to reply until they stepped into the small counseling room. "The only one at fault for what happened at the barn was your father. He chose to come here. He chose to get drunk."

Corey plopped down on a couch with Darcy

sitting beside him and Nick across from him. "I ran away and he got into trouble for that."

"The state doesn't take a child away from his parents because he ran away. Your dad wasn't caring for you. Ten-year-olds aren't meant to fend for themselves."

"But I can take care of myself. I know how."

And yet Nick had received various calls from Corey because he was afraid to be there by himself. "Do you feel safe being alone there at night?"

"He never..." Corey dropped his gaze. "He was working to take care of me."

"The whole night?" Darcy asked.

"Well, maybe." Corey hunched his shoulders.

There were so many times Nick had made up excuses for his father. "Corey, not from when you came home from school to the next morning."

The boy bent over even more as though he was trying to curl up into a ball. Darcy put her arm around Corey. "You're a child. A parent has certain responsibilities that your father wasn't living up to. He needs to get help."

"I tried to help him. He doesn't want it. I asked him to stop drinking. He stormed out of the house and was gone for a day. I never said anything else about it after that."

Nick rose from his chair and stooped in front

of Corey. "You can't fix him. He has to do that himself. You're here where you'll be safe, have three square meals a day and guidance if you run into a problem. I'm gonna be here almost every day, and you can always call me if you want to talk. Even when I'm working at the ranch, I have my cell phone with me."

"I understand that this Saturday Nick is going to give you your first riding lesson. I can remember my first time on a horse at summer camp. I was so excited to be the first one to ride into the ring that when I reached to open the gate—" she paused and waited while Corey lifted his head and peered at her "—I didn't let go while my horse went on inside. Much to my embarrassment, I was left hanging from the fence."

Corey's eyes grew round. "Did you get hurt?"

"Nope. I was just taken down a notch. So remember, when you're going through a gate, make sure you let go of it."

Corey giggled. "I know that."

"Good, because I'm going to be here to see you ride for the first time. I'll be watching. No pressure there." She ruffled his hair and hugged him.

Corey's cheeks turned beet red.

Nick stood. "We need to go, but I'm just a phone call away. Okay?"

Corey nodded.

Darcy rose at the same time Corey did. "Looking forward to seeing you tomorrow."

Corey closed the short space between him and Nick and threw his arms around him. Nick's heart swelled in his chest. "We'll continue the lesson on taking care of your horse tomorrow." Nick gave him a quick hug and stepped back, his throat tight with emotions he didn't allow himself to feel.

A few minutes later Nick stopped next to Darcy's car, tired but pleased that Corey had left them with a grin on his face. "Uncle Howard will have dinner ready at the ranch, and he wanted you to know you have an invitation to join us again tonight. I think he's taken a liking to you."

"Just your uncle?"

The heat of a blush, much like Corey's, suffused Nick's face. "I'd like you to come too. You helped me tonight, and the least I can do is give you dinner."

"Then, yes. I'll follow you to your house."

While she started her Corvette, Nick hopped into his truck and turned toward the highway. On the drive to his place he couldn't quit berating himself for prolonging the evening with Darcy. He did want to thank her for going to Dry Gulch to pick him up, but a simple thank-you would have been enough. No, he had to invite her to dinner two nights in a row.

His restless sleep last night was playing havoc with his good judgment.

As he drove onto the road that led to his house, he decided to park at his barn and check on the pregnant mare before eating. Darcy pulled up next to him.

"I'm going to see how Morning Star is doing."

"I'll come with you."

In the large foaling stall, Morning Star settled down on the straw, then immediately got back up, walked in a circle and then went down again. She did that several times. Finally on her feet, she began to push while he ran his hands over her flank.

"What's wrong?" Darcy asked him from the stall door.

"I think she's ready to deliver, but something is wrong. She's in distress. Most horses lay down to deliver." Nick retrieved his cell phone from his pocket. "I'm calling the vet."

Chapter Seven

Darcy leaned against the half door of the foaling stall as Dr. Wyatt Harrow, the veterinarian, and Nick fought to save the foal's life. Nick calmed the mare while the vet inserted his hand to reposition the foal's legs, hooves first, so it could move through the birth canal safely.

Wyatt glanced at Nick. "Okay, she should be able to push the foal out now."

Morning Star lifted her head and immediately dropped it back to the hay, her big brown eyes sliding partially closed.

His brow crinkled, Nick looked at the vet while continuing to soothe the mare. "She's exhausted. I'm not sure she can." Nick tried to coax her with a soft touch and calm words. But Morning Star didn't move while her labored breathing resonated through the stall.

"Can I help?" Darcy asked, feeling helpless and wanting to do something for the chestnut mare.

"I need some rope to pull the foal out," Wyatt said.

"Rope?" She peered at Nick.

"In the tack room on the wall."

Darcy swung around and hurried toward the front of the barn. She grabbed what the vet had requested and hoped this would work. Morning Star had been in labor to the point where she had exhausted herself. When Darcy returned, the vet quickly took the rope and began tying the foal's front hooves.

Darcy couldn't stay outside the stall watching any longer. Kneeling by Nick, she ran her hand along the horse's neck. "You're going to be okay."

At the sound of Darcy's voice close to her, Morning Star's dilated eyes shifted to Darcy. She continued her gentle stroking. Touching and comforting the mare brought back so many memories of Beauty. "If you want to help Wyatt, I can do this."

Nick moved to the vet while Darcy took over the job of consoling the mare. The last time she'd done this was when her horse had an accident while jumping a fence and died from it. She'd stayed by Beauty's side while the vet eased her death. As the memory surfaced, Darcy's throat closed. At the age of twenty-three, she'd walked away from riding. For ten years, since the horse was born, Beauty had been hers. She didn't want to see another horse die, but the foal had to come *now.*

Darcy bent closer to the mare and whispered encouraging words over and over while Wyatt and Nick struggled to pull the foal from Morning Star.

Finally it slipped free and landed in the straw. Wyatt hurriedly checked the newborn before cutting the cord while Nick wiped the afterbirth off the foal, putting it in a bucket.

"It's a filly," Wyatt said, snatching a towel to dry her off.

"You did it, Morning Star. You've got a baby girl. Way to go!" Darcy rubbed the mare that was still breathing hard.

Slowly Morning Star calmed down as Wyatt and Nick took care of the foal. She lifted her head and glanced back at her baby.

The next hour was devoted to cleaning up the mess and seeing to mother and child, both horses standing by the end, although the foal wobbled.

Wyatt gathered his black bag and stood by the stall door watching the two animals. "She's a beauty, Nick."

He grinned. "I think so too. I'm gonna call her Evening Star."

When Wyatt said *beauty*, a shaft of regret pierced Darcy's heart. If only she hadn't practiced jumping fences that day, Beauty might be alive today.

"Nice meeting you, Darcy. I'm heading home. Call me if you need me, Nick."

Pulled back to the present, Darcy erased the memory of Beauty's death and forced a grin. For years she'd loved riding horses. It was time to reclaim that love.

Nick shook the vet's hand. "I'm glad you got here so fast. I don't know how long Morning Star was in labor before we arrived."

After Wyatt left, Nick looked at her for a long moment before asking, "Okay?"

"Yes, this ended happily."

"Are you still hungry? I am. That was a lot of work."

"And you weren't even the mare in labor."

He chuckled. "Uncle Howard said he would dish up plates of food for both of us and we could warm them in the microwave."

"I'm surprised he isn't down here."

"I told him one of us needed to sleep since we're expecting a bull delivered early this morning in—" Nick checked his watch "—three hours. Besides, you were here to help if I needed it."

"Three hours?" She'd been so engrossed with

the mare she'd lost track of how long she'd been here. "What time is it?"

"Four thirty in the morning."

"Really? That went by fast."

"So are you hungry for a late dinner or early breakfast, whichever you want to call it?"

"Now that I think about it, yes, but I'll just grab a quick bite and some coffee, and then I'll head back to the Blue Bonnet Inn. Thankfully I have the luxury of sleeping in all morning."

"I'm glad one of us does." Nick strolled from the barn with Darcy beside him. As they covered the distance to the house, he took her hand.

The warmth of his palm against hers in the chill of night made her realize how much she cherished being here to help him and Morning Star.

The porch light shined, beckoning them inside where it was toasty. In the kitchen Nick microwaved each plate of baked chicken, wild rice and green beans while Darcy switched on the coffeepot.

She hoped the caffeine would keep her awake long enough to drive back to the inn. Now that the excitement of the birth was over, exhaustion was slowly weaving through her. She yawned. "Maybe I'll just take a cup with me and go before I fall asleep."

"Drink and eat some. If you don't feel awake

enough to drive, I have a spare bedroom you can use."

"I appreciate the invitation, but I'll be fine after a cup of coffee."

Twenty minutes later, after eating every bite of her tasty meal, she relaxed back in the chair. "That was delicious. Thank Howard for me." With a sigh, she rose, took her dishes to the sink and then held up the mug. "Can I top this off and take it with me? I'll bring it back to you later today."

"Yes. I'll walk you to your car."

"It's only a hundred yards away. There's no reason for both of us getting cold."

"True, but besides escorting you to your car, I'm going to check on Morning Star and her foal before I catch some shut-eye."

"Well, in that case, you can."

After putting on her overcoat, she hooked her arm through Nick's and proceeded out the back door. When she left to come to Haven, she'd never imagined that she'd be volunteering at a boys ranch because she'd discovered a cousin needed her help. Nor had she imagined someone like Nick.

At her car, she turned around to face the cowboy. "Thank you for an…interesting day."

"That's an…interesting word to describe

today." He inched closer, cupping her face, and dipped his head toward hers.

She should pull away; she was here only for a short time. But she stood her ground and met his lips with hers. He slid one hand behind her neck and held her as he deepened the kiss. A flutter in her stomach spread outward and encompassed her whole body.

When he leaned back, he smiled and then stepped away. As she drove away, he waited outside the barn, watching her leave. After going through the gate to the ranch, she stopped and looked both ways on the road into town.

The memory of his kiss swept through her as if it were happening again. Against her better judgment, she wished it could.

As she climbed out of the Corvette at the Blue Bonnet Inn, it was still dark but almost six in the morning. She used the key she'd been given to enter the large Victorian house after ten at night and came face-to-face with Carol, descending the staircase.

"I wondered where you were, but Bea told me about the problem with Corey's dad and I figured you were helping Nick out. Although there's little crime in Haven, I worry about my guests. Avery is still out, but she usually is several times a week."

"I'm sorry, Carol. I should have called to let you know. Actually Ned passed out, and we left him on his couch. I got caught up with a mare giving birth in the middle of the night."

"I'm gonna make coffee. Would you like some to take up to your room?"

"I'd love a cup. You make the best coffee I've had in a long time."

"Now, that makes my day, and it's barely started."

Darcy followed Carol to the kitchen, anticipating the aroma that saturated the house every morning. As she made the coffee, Darcy asked, "What in the world would Avery do a couple of times a week? I can't say Haven is teeming with nighttime activities." Could Avery be with Fletcher?

"Your guess is as good as mine. I suppose she could be going to Waco for more nightlife." Carol sat across from Darcy at the table. "Lana doesn't think she's the real Avery. If that's the case, we only have two months to find the real one."

"Why does she think Avery is an impostor?"

"Lana has a gut feeling something isn't right. She has observed Avery and believes she only says what she thinks we want to hear. Lana overheard that the only thing Avery worships is money. That wasn't too long after she'd told Lana that she wondered if a church service would help her deal with all the things she missed out on because she didn't know her grandfather. All she wanted to do was honor him."

"And yet she's close to Fletcher, who doesn't want to honor Cyrus's wish to give his land to the boys ranch."

"Yeah, that's what I've been wondering too. What if she's working behind the scenes to find a way to break the will? It sure would be easier if she wasn't the real Avery. Dealing with Fletcher is one thing. Dealing with Cyrus's closest living relative is more complicated." Carol walked to the coffeepot and filled two mugs.

Interesting. Maybe she could see if Lana needed any help proving whether or not Avery was the real one. "I've seen the good the boys ranch does. I'd hate to see that change." And if she was the real Avery, maybe she could be persuaded to legally fight whatever Fletcher was doing to ruin the provisions of the will.

Carol handed her a mug. "You and me both. A strip mall isn't what Cyrus really wanted the ranch to be used for."

Darcy rose. "I'll be seeing Lana this afternoon at the boys ranch. But if I don't want to miss working with Corey, I'd better catch some z's."

Darcy sipped the coffee and headed for the

staircase. In the entry hall she spied Avery mounting the steps to the second floor. Had she been with Fletcher? Were they scheming to take the boys ranch away? The idea that her biological father could do something like that sickened her.

On Saturday Nick stood in the middle of the corral as three boys rode for the first time—Corey, Mikey and Miguel, all only a few years apart in age, relatively new to the ranch and living in the second wing. Corey on Ginger led the group.

"Mikey, you're holding the rein too tight." When the blond-headed boy adjusted his grip, Nick added, "That's right. If you all keep this up, I'll take you on a trail ride." He moved to the side and lounged against the fence.

Corey pumped his arm in the air while Mikey grinned, displaying the gap where his two front teeth used to be, and Miguel cheered.

"I hoped I'd get here before Corey started his riding lesson." Darcy's soft voice floated to him from behind.

He shot her a glance over his shoulder. "I wondered if you were coming."

"You wouldn't believe it. I had two flat tires when I came out of the inn."

"Who changed them?"

"Me with some help from Clarence and Slim. My car hasn't given me any trouble until this trip." She opened the gate and entered the corral. "What I don't understand is two at once unless someone did it deliberately."

Lately so many things had happened to people involved with the boys ranch. Could it be the saboteur who had messed with her tires? Why? She didn't live here. But then, she'd been at the ranch every day this past week.

"What did I miss?" Darcy asked.

"About nineteen laps around the perimeter. All three are naturals, especially Corey."

"He's a sharp learner. Each day I work with him reading, he's a little better than the day before. I think all he needed was someone to listen to him and practice."

He was glad to see her. He'd missed her the last two days at the boys ranch and when he had spotted her before that, he'd felt awkward after the kiss they shared. He shouldn't have kissed her. She would be leaving at the end of the month, but her presence that night had been like returning to the fortified base after a skirmish. "So what have you been up to since we last talked?"

"Besides tutoring, I've been helping Lana track down information on Avery Culpepper.

Lana told me on Wednesday that Avery doesn't have any of the Culpepper family coloring."

"You don't think the one in town is the right Avery?"

"If she isn't, then that might hurt the boys ranch because of the provision in the will."

His gaze still trained on the riders, Nick straightened. "What if Fletcher recruited a fake Avery in order to mess up the stipulations that have to be met by March?"

"Just a sec." Darcy came into the paddock. "I found out a few details, like the fact that Avery was born on February 2. Since she is staying at the Blue Bonnet Inn, I'm going to try to get to know her and test her on the facts I've discovered."

"And she won't get suspicious?"

"I'm a lawyer. I know how to interview a person to get what I want."

"I'll have to remember that. Do you want to go on a trail ride with us?"

She grinned, her blue eyes twinkling. "I would love to. I haven't ridden in years. I need to start again."

"Do I need to give you a lesson?" Nick asked with a chuckle.

"I think I'll be okay. How are Morning Star and Evening Star doing?"

"Great. Morning Star is a natural mother. I'm

glad this foal lived." Nick approached the circling riders. "Stop by the gate. We're gonna go for a trail ride. I want to show Darcy the ranch. Okay?"

Cheers rose from the boys. Corey grinned from ear to ear—its sight infectious. This past week he had lived at the barn in his spare time, doing whatever Flint or Nick would let him. Corey had even told Nick that he wanted to be a farrier like he was. For a moment Nick had thrust back his shoulders and stood up tall, as though he were a proud dad and his son had declared he wanted to follow in his footsteps. Then reality swept the thought out of his mind. His life wasn't an example for a child to follow. He was barely making a living and he was filled with anger at his father that he'd never been able to shake.

"Nick, are you okay?" Darcy's soft Southern voice pulled him back to the present, where three boys were staring at him.

"I'm fine. I'll be right back with our horses." Nick had already selected the horses he would use. There was a creek he wanted to show her.

In ten minutes he returned to the paddock, leading two mares. He loved seeing the grins on the boys' faces, especially Corey's. Each day he saw signs that Corey was fitting right in and starting to relax and enjoy himself. At least now

Nick didn't have to worry about the child. He could be near him and keep an eye on him—be the big brother Doug had been for Corey.

After giving Darcy a leg up, he swung into the saddle. "I have a special place I want to show y'all. I'll be in the lead. Darcy will be in the rear."

For January the day was beautiful, not a cloud in the sky, the temperature in the mid-fifties. Corey rode next to Nick, smiling the whole time.

"How's school going, partner?"

"Okay. Aiden's in my class, and he's been showing me around."

"I'm glad you're making friends. Any problems?"

For a long moment Corey didn't reply.

"You can tell me. It'll remain between us if that's what you want."

"There's one boy in wing three. Jasper. I saw him hide Billy's backpack the other day right before we were supposed to get on the school bus. Billy was freaking out."

"What did you do?"

"I found the backpack. I don't think Jasper liked that."

"He can be the class clown at times. Usually he plays pranks, most of the time in fun. Sometimes he goes too far."

"Why?"

"I don't know for sure. Maybe for attention."

Corey sat up even straighter in the saddle. "Then I'll make friends with him. We had a kid like that at my old school. That's what I did there. Doug told me when I started school I should look out for the ones who need a friend."

"He's younger. You'll be a good role model for Jasper. Doug's advice is right on." Helping others would also give Corey something to do to take his mind off his own problems.

"Yeah, Doug was a great big brother. I miss him."

"So do I, Corey."

Twenty minutes later, the group arrived at the stream, which was partially shaded by trees that retained their leaves in the winter.

Nick dismounted and turned to the boys. "You saw how I got off my horse. Y'all do the same thing and then tie the reins to a bush or small tree so the animals can graze while you look around."

"How long can we explore?" Corey slid off his mount.

"You can't go too far. Keep me in sight. I'll give a shout when I want you to come back."

As the boys moved away, sticking together, Darcy stopped at Nick's side. "Mikey had a little trouble keeping his horse from wanting to eat as he walked, but otherwise they all did great."

"Riding is good for both them and the horses. This ranch is big and has a lot of places they can explore."

She looked around. "This would be a fun place to have a picnic."

"That's something we could do when the weather permits."

Shielding her eyes, she shifted her attention to him. "You'll be able to. A cold front is coming through tomorrow, and I won't be here after the end of the month."

Yeah, he had to remember that. He was attracted to her, and there was no future for them. She'd made it clear she loved her home. Long-distance relationships didn't work. Too many barriers. "Who knows? Weather can change rapidly here in the winter. The other ranch site wasn't nearly as big and didn't have the opportunities this one has, like the ability to have a picnic in a place like this. I'm going to talk to Flint about having trail rides on the weekend. Not a bad way to keep an eye on what's happening on the ranch too."

Darcy tilted her head. "You know, back in Mobile I was good at organizing fund-raisers. I've been thinking the past few days, it would be fun to do a small one for the boys ranch. If I were staying longer, I'd go all out. The money could go to equipment and other items this place needs."

"Sounds good. You need to talk to Bea—"

"Nick, come quick," Corey shouted, about two hundred yards away.

Nick ran toward the boys, who were staring down an incline. It looked like they were all right, but the urgency in Corey's voice had been clear. Something was wrong.

He halted with Darcy right beside him. "What's wrong?"

Corey pointed a shaky hand down the slope.

Nick stepped forward. Below, a cow was down on the ground, trying to get up but not able to. "Darcy, can you take the boys back to the ranch, wait for Wyatt to come and then show him here?"

"Yes."

He started down the incline. "I'll call the vet and stay with the cow."

"I don't wanna leave. I found her. You might need me." Corey stood his ground.

Darcy put her hand on his shoulder. "C'mon. I might get lost going back to the barn. I need y'all to guide me."

"Oh, o-kay."

Darcy waved at him as Nick knelt next to the cow and saw that it had a broken leg. If Wyatt had to put the animal down, he didn't want the boys to see it. And once again Darcy had been here to help him. He didn't want to get too used to that. She was leaving soon.

Chapter Eight

Darcy rode back to the barn for the second time that day to let the boys know that Wyatt would be able to cast the cow's leg and save her.

With Flint's assistance, the cow had been moved to a board and then loaded on a trailer. Wyatt and Nick were coming back with the animal, hoping to keep her calm. It was Darcy's job to put the boys' fears to rest. She arrived at the barn a few minutes before the men.

The second Corey saw her he ran toward her and met her at the back door. "What happened? Is she okay?"

"Yes, Wyatt will be putting a cast on her leg. They're coming right behind me," she said as the other two boys skidded to a stop next to Corey.

Relief transformed each child's serious expression into joy.

When Bea and Lana approached, they interrupted the boys' plans to help the cow.

Bea directed her look at Corey. "Y'all will not do anything unless the vet says so. You three can fix up a stall for the cow with Johnny." She waved for the older teenager to join them. "Johnny, these guys are going to help you clean out the big stall so Wyatt can use it to work on the cow."

He nodded and waited for the trio to follow him. The teen stuttered as he told the boys what they needed to get, but the young ones were oblivious to it.

Bea watched the group head to the stall with tools. "Johnny has been such a big help to Wyatt. He'd rather spend his time at the barn than at the house. If I let him, he'd sleep down here."

"A lot of them would," Lana said. "There's something about animals that allow the kids to heal. That's why this place is so important to the boys and has to stay open."

Darcy waited until the children disappeared inside the stall. "Speaking of the ranch, I've discovered a couple of pieces of information about Avery after doing some digging. If I can catch her in a lie about one of them, that might prove she's an imposter. But you need to be prepared. It's possible she is the real Avery."

Lana sighed. "I hope not. This ranch is too important for the boys to lose it at the last minute. We still have a couple of people to track down, like Gabe Everett's grandfather. Then there's Morton Mason—"

Darcy spied Wyatt entering the barn right behind Bea.

Bea interrupted Lana. "With everything happening today, I haven't had a chance to tell you, Lana, that I found an address for Carolina Mason, though no phone number or email. So I'll be writing her a letter about the boys ranch's anniversary party. Hopefully she knows where her great-uncle is. If so, we'll be set with that original resident."

Wyatt began to open the other half of the front entrance, but he halted, the color washing from his face as he stared at Bea's. Then, before Bea had a chance to say anything, he pivoted and hurriedly unlatched the door. But Darcy had seen his look of regret—and something else. A flash of anger?

Darcy spent the next hour keeping the boys quiet as they watched Nick, Johnny and Wyatt put a cast on the back leg of the cow. Flint kept her down and as calm as possible.

"Boys, it's lunchtime," Bea announced to the three younger ones.

Corey turned to the director. "We want to stay and make sure she's okay. Please."

Bea exchanged a look with Lana and Darcy. "Wyatt is almost finished. Come up to the house and eat and then you can return and assist Nick and Flint."

Flint stuck his head out of the open top half of the stall door. "I'll let you three take turns keeping an eye on the cow with Johnny. She's going to have a calf in about a month. We want to make sure they are both all right. Is that a deal?"

Corey's eyes popped wide. All three kids happily agreed. "Do you want to join us?" Bea asked Darcy.

She peeked into the large stall. Like the boys, she wanted to stay and help, but Nick had already put the last of the plaster on the cast.

"Bring us back something to eat. Wyatt and I will be with old Bessie until you get back from lunch," Nick said to Darcy.

"Bessie?" Did they name the cows in their herd?

"Yup. My name for her." He gave her a grin and a wink. "Aren't all cows named Bessie?"

"I think there's a Flossie and Elsie."

He laughed. "I've worked up quite an appetite. Lifting a cow ain't easy work."

"I'll remember that." Darcy gathered up the boys, and the group left the barn.

Once the kids were outside, they sprinted toward the house, leaving Lana, Bea and Darcy in their dust.

Lana chuckled. "I can't believe they don't want to walk with us."

"Next they'll be calling us old fogies," Bea muttered, "and at the moment I feel that way."

"Why?" Darcy asked.

"Did you see Wyatt's face when he heard about me writing a letter to Carolina Mason?"

Lana's forehead crinkled. "Yes. Didn't those two date?"

"Yes, and she abruptly left town three years ago. I'm not sure why, and I don't think Wyatt knows either."

"If anyone should know, it would be you or Carol." Lana mounted the steps to the front porch.

"I'm discovering that while staying at the Blue Bonnet Inn," Darcy said. "I feel like I know a lot of people in this town, and I haven't even met them. Carol knows everyone." And through it all, what Darcy had discovered about her biological father wasn't good.

After eating lunch, Darcy made up a plate of food for Nick while Lana did the same for Flint and Logan, who had joined his dad. Johnny and Corey had already headed down to the barn while Mikey and Miguel finished their hamburgers.

As the group left the house, Mikey tripped on

the stairs and cut his leg. Lana handed Darcy one plate and gave the other to Miguel.

Lana knelt next to Mikey, tears running down the seven-year-old's face, and examined the injury. "We'll be down after I clean this and get a bandage for him."

Darcy and Miguel continued their trek. Inside the barn, Flint stood at the entrancc of the tack room while Cowboy barked over and over at the closed back door.

She passed Flint his food. "Miguel has Logan's. Y'all eat. I'll see what Cowboy is upset about."

"Thanks. If he doesn't stop, I'll take him home." He held up their plates. "After we eat. We're starving."

"Is Nick with the cow?"

"Yeah."

"Are Corey and Johnny there too?"

Flint nodded as he took a bite.

"Miguel, please give this to Nick while I see about Cowboy."

When she neared the black Lab, he scratched at the door, looked back at her and then barked again. Maybe all he wanted to do was pee. He never ran off, so he should be all right. She exited with the dog. Cowboy charged around the side. She hurried after him in case she'd been wrong and he was escaping.

The scents of gasoline and smoke laced the air. Her steps quickened as she rounded the corner, the black Lab yelping at the gray smoke and flames eating their way up the barn.

For one, two seconds she stared at the fire. Then her gaze fell on a gasoline can nearby, cap off and knocked over.

As she dug for her cell phone, she whirled around and raced to get the people and animals out before it was too late.

Nick leaned against the stall door while Corey stroked the cow. Johnny had gone to get Bessie something to eat. Unlike a horse, a cow could be content lying on the ground, resting and munching on grass. They rarely ran around, which meant the leg should heal fine.

"Get out! There's a fire!" Darcy's warning instantly invaded the tranquil moment.

Nick jerked upright and swung around. "Where?"

She hastened to him and pointed. "That side of the barn in the middle. I smelled gasoline and checked it out."

Flint ran out of the tack room with Logan and Miguel, gesturing for the boys to leave and saying, "Go get help at the house." Then Flint asked Darcy, "Have you called 911?"

Darcy took deep breaths, her chest rising and falling rapidly. "Yes, but I didn't let anyone at the main house know about the fire yet."

"Nick, get everyone out. I'm calling Bea and shutting the front doors." Flint pulled out his cell phone and strode away.

"Darcy, open the stall doors on that side and wave your arms to get the horses to run out the back." Nick turned to Corey and Johnny. "Y'all try to direct the horses into the corral where you were riding this morning. Don't worry if any of them get away. We'll find them later."

Already on his feet, Johnny rushed out of the stall, but Corey, hand still on the cow, didn't move. "What about Bessie?"

"You don't worry about her. I will. Go. Get out. Now."

Nick stared at the cow. The cast was hard. Maybe she would walk out okay. He needed rope and possibly someone to hoist Bessie to her feet and move her outside. First, he had to see to the mare stabled on this side.

Smoke began to fill the barn, its insidious smell invading every crevice. Flames ate at the outside of the wooden wall.

Nick opened the stall door and tried to coax Ginger out. Her eyes wild-looking, she backed away from the exit, her nose flaring. "Easy, girl. You'll be all right," Nick said in a soft, calm tone.

After a long thirty seconds, Ginger finally shot out of the stall and raced for the back door. Nick glanced out to make sure all the horses were accounted for in the corral. He was missing one—a black gelding.

Flint was occupied with organizing the staff and teenage boys to hose down what they could until the fire department arrived. Nick would have to take care of Bessie and check to see if the gelding had gone toward the front because his stall door was opened wide.

As Nick hurried back in for Bessie, the big black horse charged toward him. He dove to the side and the gelding ran outside.

Darcy quickened her step to him. "He was the last one. The stalls are empty except for the cow's. What do you need me to do?"

"Hold the rope while I get her to stand and then we'll walk her out."

After securing Bessie with the rope, he gave it to Darcy. As she stood in front, trying to coax the cow, he urged Bessie to stand, no mean feat with a cast on. Once Bessie was up, Darcy led her toward the exit.

Nick pivoted one last time to make sure the barn was clear, but the smoke had grown denser.

He could hardly see the other end. A beam crashed down, flames engulfing it.

"Nick, get out," Darcy shouted from the back door.

He hastened out the exit as the sound of the building beginning to collapse drowned out the crackling of the fire. Grabbing Darcy's hand, he put distance between them and the barn, the blaze quickly spreading up one side and across the roof.

Two fire trucks barreled down the gravel road toward them.

"It's too late to save the barn, but at least they can keep the fire from getting out of control and destroying more of the ranch," Flint said to Nick when he reached him.

The loud whinnies from the nearest corral vied with the noise of the fire. The scent of smoke hung heavily, and the staff began steering the boys to the house. Some of them were crying, others stunned.

When Corey didn't want to leave, Darcy walked to him and said something that Nick couldn't hear, but Corey nodded and trailed after the others.

Nick glanced at the paddock twenty yards away. "Should we move the horses farther away?"

Flint nodded. "Just in case the wind picks up.

Let's put them in the pasture on the other side of the main house for the time being."

Nick stared at the nearest ranch structure, his eyes watering, his throat burning from the smell. "Are there any halters and reins in the storage barn?"

"No, because we're using this one as our primary barn for horses."

"Then I'll head to my ranch and bring enough back to move the horses. I need to park my truck farther away anyway. It shouldn't take me too long."

"Go. There isn't anything we can do now but pray."

"I'll help you, Nick," Darcy said beside him.

For the first time in years, Nick sent up a silent prayer that no one was hurt and nothing was damaged except for the barn. It could be rebuilt with the insurance money.

Darcy hopped into the cab of his pickup with two bottles of water, and they pulled away from the chaos at the boys ranch. He let out a long breath, clasped the drink and downed half of it. "Thanks. That's what I needed."

"That's the first fire I've been in, and I never want to repeat that experience. I had trouble with that black gelding. All I could do was pray he found his way outside the barn. I opened his stall and barely jumped out of his way."

"I noticed even in the corral he was more agitated than the other horse."

"I'm glad we were able to get Bessie out. Corey was so worried about her."

Nick drove through the gates of his ranch. "What did you say to him to get him to leave with the others?"

"I promised him I would make sure the barn was rebuilt even better than the one that burned."

Nick frowned. "How can you make him that promise? You'll be leaving in three weeks."

"I'll get the town behind it. As I told you earlier, I've had a lot of experience with fund-raisers. When the people see what the boys lost, they'll help. Instead of using what we raise for equipment, we can use it to rebuild the barn. A fund-raiser could also show Fletcher Phillips that Haven supports the ranch."

"He's probably the one behind the fire."

Darcy gasped. "You really think that?"

"If gasoline was used, it was arson. It has to be someone who doesn't like the boys ranch. That fits Fletcher."

"How about Ned? He was furious that Corey was taken away from him."

Nick parked by his barn. "That was the alcohol talking. If Ned ever stopped drinking, he might be the father Corey needs. I know that's most likely not going to happen, but I can hope it does."

"You knew him when he wasn't an alcoholic?"

"Years ago, when they lived in Haven." According to Uncle Howard, Nick's father had been a better man too, before Nick's mother died. "Believe me, I know that if he doesn't stop drinking, he'll keep doing what he's been doing."

"Are you talking about your father? I got the impression that he had a drinking problem based on something you said before."

For a moment, he considered telling her everything about his father, but the words wouldn't come. Confiding in Darcy was a risk he didn't dare take.

Chapter Nine

Darcy slipped into Lila's Café to meet Avery for coffee before going to the church to discuss the fund-raiser. The fire department had confirmed it was arson, which didn't surprise her. Gasoline cans didn't just lie around the boys ranch.

She was so glad she'd started thinking about doing a fund-raiser because the boys would need something positive to focus on and to look forward to. She'd talked to Bea about the idea and the director had encouraged her. Any money they received helped. She paused by the entrance and scanned the restaurant for Avery. Darcy spotted the young woman sitting at a table—with Fletcher. The two seemed deep in a conversation. Good time to break up the pair. She threaded her way through the crowded café and slid into a chair.

"I'm sorry I'm late. Carol stopped me right

before I left the inn." Darcy swung her attention from Avery to Fletcher.

"I'm Darcy Hill, visiting Haven for the month." She held out her hand to her birth father.

Fletcher shook it. "I'm Fletcher Phillips. I'm not staying. Avery told me she was meeting you for coffee. I understand you were at the fire yesterday at the boys ranch."

Darcy nodded. "It was arson."

"I heard that this morning at church."

"I told Fletcher how ragged you looked when you returned to the inn last night. I would have been hysterical if I'd been caught in a fire," Avery said.

"Thankfully we had plenty of time to get the animals and people out of there."

"I've been saying ever since the ranch was set up for this purpose that something bad like this would happen. I wouldn't be surprised if it was one of those *boys*. We're fortunate that the wind wasn't too strong or it could have spread—possibly even caused a major wildfire affecting the whole town."

Darcy gritted her teeth, trying not to say anything she would regret, but she couldn't keep quiet. "But it didn't, and it wasn't one of the kids."

"How do you know that?"

Disappointed in her biological father, Darcy asked, "How do you know it was one of them?"

His sharp gaze cut through her as he rose. "It's been interesting talking to you, Ms. Hill. Avery, we'll talk some more later."

She giggled. "I'd like that, Fletcher. I want to move forward."

Move forward doing what? Upsetting the plans for the Culpepper ranch?

Each morning, when Avery came down for breakfast, Darcy made a point of speaking to her. Nothing Avery had said so far had sent up a red flag suggesting she wasn't the real Avery Culpepper, but Darcy hoped she could discover something. "I've seen him pick you up a couple of times this week. Are you two serious?"

For a few seconds, the woman's pupils dilated. "Like dating?"

"That's what I've heard."

Avery tossed back her head and laughed. "He's the lawyer for my grandfather's inheritance. Haven has a nest of gossipers spreading untruths."

"Then why do you stay here? Aren't you from—Dallas?"

"To honor my grandfather's wishes. I may not have known him, but family is important to me."

While the waitress took their order, Darcy clenched her fists so tightly that her fingernails dug into her palms. Talking to Avery would require all her restraint. "It is for me too. I understand you were a foster child. Do you remember your real parents?"

"Vaguely. My mother died when I was really young and my father, John, Cyrus's son, followed a few years later. That's when I became part of the foster care system, but I had a nice set of foster parents."

"I was adopted when I was a baby. When I found out, I asked my parents if my birthday was really in April. They assured me it was. Did your foster parents know when your real one was?"

"Of course."

"When's your birthday? Anytime around mine?"

"Mine isn't until M—" Avery glanced down at her watch. "Look at the time. I have another appointment, and I'm gonna be late." She pushed to her feet. "We'll talk another time."

Avery scurried toward the exit, leaving Darcy with her bill when their drinks came. Whether Avery had been about to say March or May didn't make any difference since the real Avery Culpepper was born on February 2. Darcy didn't even get a chance to ask her what her biological mother's name was. Maybe she'd find another time to quiz her, but today at the fund-raising meeting at the church, she would let Lana know what the fake "Avery" said. Evidence was piling up against the women who claimed she was the granddaughter of Cyrus Culpepper.

When the waitress arrived with coffee to go, Darcy paid the bill and left so she wouldn't be late for the meeting.

Ten minutes later she entered the large classroom at the Haven Community Church. Only a few people—Nick, Flint and Lana—were there, but it was still early. She would need all the help she could get to pull off this fund-raiser in another week. She wanted to be in town for it.

Darcy sat between Lana and Nick. "Do y'all know if anyone else is coming? Carol will be here." Sitting next to Nick gave her the confidence she would be able to successfully make the fund-raiser work.

"My uncle Howard is, but he may be a little late."

"Bea and Katie are coming and Pastor Andrew will be here after he returns a phone call. Also Heath and Josie." Flint grinned. "They're getting married in a few weeks and meeting with the pastor afterward."

"That's great. I know this is rushed, but when I discussed this with Nick—" she paused, her glance falling on him "—my extensive background in fund-raising seemed the best way to help. If this is successful, hopefully you can have more of them."

"That's what I'm hoping." A petite, very pregnant woman with long, auburn hair and brown eyes stood at the doorway with a tall man wearing a Texas Ranger star pinned to his shirt.

"Come in." Darcy rose and faced the couple. "I'm Darcy Hill. You must be Josie Markham and Heath Grayson." She shook hands with both of them.

"Yes," Josie said and took a chair across from Darcy.

"I understand congratulations are in order. I really appreciate y'all helping when you're also planning your wedding and having a baby."

"Well, the baby's not due for eight more weeks unless it decides to come early. I especially want to see what you do because I'm hoping the Lone Star Cowboy League will start a ranch for girls."

As Lana asked Josie about the wedding, which was going to be small, Bea, Katie, Carol and the pastor came into the room. Katie slid a glance at Pastor Andrew as she sat next to him. When he looked at Katie, her cheeks reddened. Darcy had heard rumors about Katie having a crush on Pastor Andrew.

Nick bent toward her and whispered, "We should go ahead and start. I'll fill in my uncle on the plans."

The brush of air along her neck sent goose bumps down her arms. The memory of his kiss instantly flooded her mind. "Okay," she managed to say while her heartbeat accelerated.

"When Carol, Bea and I started talking about a fund-raiser, we thought it would be fun for the kids to show off some of their riding skills. I know that some are practicing their showmanship. We could also have competitions like barrel racing and roping. I was hoping I could leave that up to Nick, Flint and Howard since y'all work with the boys. We could have food for sale, charge an admission fee and also give tours of the new ranch."

"We can use the arena between the burnt barn and the storage one. But where will people sit? And, although the arena is covered, we'll have to consider the weather for stuff like the food," Flint said.

Pastor Andrew waved his hand. "I have a solution for where people will sit. I know a church in Waco that has portable bleachers we can borrow. A friend is the pastor there."

"We can set up big tents where the food will be served. If it's colder than predicted, we can possibly get some heaters," Darcy said.

Flint looked at Nick. "Didn't you ride in the rodeo as a teen? Could you demonstrate roping and tying a calf? Maybe invite members of the audience to try their hand at it?"

"Sure. Although what the kids will do isn't really a rodeo, we should have someone here dress up as a clown and be out in the ring keeping an eye on the activities as well as acting as an emcee."

As everyone offered suggestions, Darcy grew excited about the fund-raiser. Once most of the program was agreed upon and people were put in charge of different activities, she said, "This will be a great opportunity to show everyone what the boys ranch is really all about and how people can come together to support the place. When we're through next Saturday, hopefully we'll have convinced any naysayers about why the ranch should be here. I'm personally going to invite Fletcher Phillips to the event."

"He won't come," Bea said immediately.

Howard walked into the room. "Challenge him. He usually can't resist that."

"Thanks, Howard. I'll do that. Now, some folks might not attend the outdoor event, but in the evening we could have a ladies' choice dance, possibly in the arena after it is cleaned from the show."

"I have a better idea," Pastor Andrew said. "How about we have it here at the church in our hall? There would be more room, and I have a group of women who would love to organize it, especially if it's a ladies' choice dance."

Heath held Josie's hand. "I know a Texas Ranger in my office who sometimes works as a DJ. I can see if he's free."

"If he isn't available, I can do it in a pinch," Howard said.

Darcy wrapped up the meeting once all the members had assignments. "We'll meet back here on Wednesday evening. Thanks, Carol, for volunteering to get the word out about the fund-raiser."

"I'll do that and more. Clarence will help too." Carol accompanied the pastor and Katie as they left the room.

Bea hung back and pulled Darcy to the side. "We need to make sure this fund-raiser goes off without a hitch. I got a call from the Texas Department of Family and Protective Services. They're concerned about safety at the ranch, especially after the fire. They are launching an investigation. I told them about the planned fund-raiser, and they stressed that nothing bad better happen to call more attention to the place."

"I'll let Nick and Flint know. Perhaps a call from Heath, letting them know about what the police are doing, will ease their concerns."

"Good idea, Darcy. I'll talk to Heath and the sheriff." Bea hurried out of the room.

Darcy shut her notebook and faced Lana, Flint and Nick. "I have my work cut out for me in the next week."

Lana chuckled. "She was just complaining on Friday that she wished the kids were out of school so she could help them more than she already does," Lana told Flint and Nick. "Now you have something to do, Darcy, and I'll join in where I can."

"Before I forget to tell you, I had coffee with Avery right before the meeting," Darcy said. "The woman I talked to didn't know when the real Avery's birthday was. She started to say a month other than February but stopped herself and hurried out of the café. If she went into foster care, she would know when she was born. It would be in the records. She would need it for school."

"So she isn't the real Avery. Now what?"

"Let me do some more digging and then we can confront her for answers. She should be able to get a copy of her birth certificate if she's the real Avery, so if she can't, that's an indication she's an imposter. And we can call her on it."

"Then we should start looking for the real one. The town still has to meet Cyrus's requirement for the boys to stay at the Culpepper ranch."

"I'll start looking quietly."

"What are you two plotting?" Flint asked.

"The fake Avery's downfall and we need to do it soon. Time is running out to find the real one." Lana linked her arm through his. "See you tomorrow, Darcy."

Nick put the chairs back at the tables where they belonged. "The meeting went well. I hope it generates a lot of interest in the community. The boys ranch can always use donations and volunteers."

"And Josie hopes someone will start a girls ranch. Now that's something I would love to be part of." The second she said it, she realized that it wouldn't be possible for her, but maybe she could do something similar where she lived. It wouldn't have the feel of a Western ranch, but a farm could work.

"C'mon. I'll walk you to your car."

"I didn't use my car. Today was beautiful, and I enjoyed the exercise. I'm praying this will be what next Saturday is like."

"Then I'll drive you to the Blue Bonnet Inn."

"How about taking a walk with me? Bea told me that the Lone Star Cowboy League sponsors the boys ranch. Are you a member?"

Nick opened the door for her and then followed her outside. "Yes, although not as active as Gabe Everett, the president, or Tanner Barstow, the vice president. The Lone Star Cowboy League serves the whole county."

"Even Waco?"

"Yes, the secretary of the league is Seth Jacobs. He has a prosperous ranch and lives in Waco. What I like about the meetings—" he paused, smiling "—that is, when I attend—is talking with other ranchers around McLennan County."

"I can understand that. What affects one rancher could impact another." Darcy glanced at Lila's Café and gestured toward it. "Besides having coffee with Avery there, I officially met Fletcher today."

The only response Nick gave her was a frown.

"He won't be too happy when I uncover that Avery's a fraud."

"I heard you talking to Lana. So you're sure?"

"Ninety-nine percent, but I'll do some double-checking before I say anything."

"I'd love to see Fletcher's face when that happens."

"Maybe the man really feels the boys ranch isn't good for Haven."

Nick started to reply, but Darcy stopped, faced him and touched his mouth. "We know it is. Next Saturday I intend to *show* Fletcher it is."

"You really think he'll come?"

"I'm gonna make it impossible for him to say no. Once he sees how much the ranch is helping the children, I refuse to believe the man will continue his legal battle to shut it down." Because half of her genes were his and she wanted him to be more like her adopted father.

"You'll be disappointed, Darcy." He stepped closer. "But what I like about you is your fighting spirit to the end. You don't give up easily."

His nearness sent her pulse racing. "I have a feeling you don't either." Her breaths shortened.

"No. If I did I would have walked away from my family ranch when I came home from serving in the army."

"Why? What I saw of your place was nice."

He lowered his head closer to her. "It was neglected for years, but my uncle and I have been slowly turning it around."

His scent swirled around her, mingling with the smells carried on the breeze. She wanted him to kiss her again. But then a car on Main turned onto Third Street, honking as it went by.

Nick backed away, his cheeks red.

"Who was that?" Darcy brushed her hair away from her face, her hand trembling slightly.

"Gabe Everett. Probably going to the boys ranch, which is where I need to be."

"Yeah, I have some investigating to do. I can walk the rest of the way by myself. Haven isn't big enough to get lost in." She looked both ways on Main and then crossed the street.

She should thank Gabe for honking. Kissing

Nick in the middle of the town wasn't what she'd come to Haven for. Her days here were ticking down, and she needed to find a time to tell Fletcher he was her biological father, because she still wanted to know about her biological family.

Late Monday afternoon, Nick left the stall in the old barn where Bessie was staying, expecting Corey and several others to visit after Darcy tutored them. Between his chores at the Flying Eagle, working with Flint on the animals that would be in the rodeo and instructing Corey and the other boys participating in a beginner version of barrel racing, he probably wouldn't see much of Darcy until the meeting on Wednesday.

That was a good thing. At least he was trying to convince himself it was. But for the past twenty-four hours, since he had almost kissed her again, he couldn't get her out of his mind. She lived hundreds of miles away. On several occasions she had talked about her stay in Haven ending at the end of January. He had to get through the next few weeks, and then life would get back to normal.

He headed to the entrance to wait for the younger barrel racers. Flint was working with the older group. He spied four boys walking toward him, but Corey wasn't one of them. His cell phone rang. Quickly he answered Bea's call. "Nick, I need you up at my office."

"Is something wrong? Is Corey all right?"

"Corey is fine and still with Darcy."

"I'll be there."

After letting Flint know he was going to Bea's office, Nick hastened to the main house. He knocked on Bea's door, heard her tell him to come in and then he entered, surprised to find Darcy sitting in one of two chairs in front of the director's desk. It must be about the fund-raiser. Had Fletcher caused some kind of ruckus concerning it? He took a seat, sharing a puzzled look with Darcy.

"Darcy, is Corey with Katie?"

She nodded.

"He is new here, and I don't know him well enough to tell him that his father was in a car wreck half an hour ago. He was pronounced dead at the scenc of thc onc-car accident. I was hoping one of you would break the news to Corey."

"I will," both Nick and Darcy said at the same time.

He slanted a glance at Darcy, pleased she wanted to help. "We'll do it together."

Bea heaved a sigh. "Good. He needs people around him who he's familiar with. While you talk with him, I'm going to let his houseparents know. Abby and John will inform the other boys in Corey's wing."

"Where was the wreck?"

"A mile from here."

"So he could have been on his way here." Darcy's voice wavered.

"That's what I think." Bea rose and headed for the door. "I'll send Corey in here."

"Do you think Ned was going to cause another scene here?" Nick asked the second the director left.

"I want to think that Ned was coming to apologize."

"How do you manage to look on the bright side in the middle of all of this?"

"Because it gives me hope."

He wished he could see things her way, but knowing Ned as he did, he doubted that was the case. "Possibly unrealistic hope? You must get disappointed a lot."

"Yes, sometimes I am, but I don't want to go through life only looking at the negative in a person."

The sound of footsteps nearing the office silenced Nick's reply. He hadn't started out so pessimistic, but during the years he'd lived with an alcoholic father, he'd been disillusioned too many times when his dad had promised to do better and never did.

After Corey entered the room, Nick closed the door and pulled up a third chair while the child sank down onto his seat. Corey's teeth bit into his bottom lip. His gaze flitted from Darcy to Nick and then back. The child knew something was wrong.

Darcy leaned forward and took Corey's hand. "Corey, we have some bad news. Miss Bea was just notified that your father was in a wreck. I'm sorry to tell you, but he didn't survive."

Corey sat, silent, staring at Darcy as though he hadn't heard what she said.

"Nick and I are here for you."

The boy swung his attention to Nick. "Was he drunk?"

"I don't know. He was coming to see you." Nick shifted his gaze to Darcy briefly and decided he would believe the best of Ned. "He was only a mile away from here. He, no doubt, wanted to ask for your forgiveness."

"Why did he come last time?" Corey swallowed hard. "He embarrassed me. He was always yelling at me."

"Some people drink for courage. They think alcohol helps them to do what they need to. They haven't figured out that it actually hurts their cause. That doesn't mean he didn't love you. He yelled because he was frustrated, more with himself than with anyone." As he said those words to Corey, he began to wonder if his father had felt that way. Had Dad loved him and just hadn't known how to show it?

Corey chewed on his bottom lip, fighting the grief sweeping over him. Nick knew that look. At his dad's funeral he'd worn the same expression, not sure how to feel. Relieved or sad or both? Corey dropped his chin, clenching his hands together in his lap.

Nick didn't know what else to say. He hadn't handled his dad's death well, so how could he counsel another kid experiencing the same thing? He connected with Darcy's gaze. Maybe she would be better at it. Her look of sympathy, which suggested she knew what Corey was going through—what Nick had gone through too—swamped him. She couldn't know. She came from a supportive family who made her feel loved.

Corey raised his head, his eyes shiny. "What's gonna happen to me?"

"You'll stay here for a while. Nothing should change right now." He didn't want the child to go into the foster care system, possibly shuffled from one home to the next. Corey already had a hard time believing anyone loved him. But, for so many reasons, Nick didn't think he would be a good father figure for the boy. Maybe there was a relative that would come forward.

Darcy clasped his upper arm. "That shouldn't concern you right now. I'm a lawyer. I'll look into it for you."

"You will?" Corey asked with wonderment.

"Sure." She smiled. "Anything for you. You've got people who care about you now." She peered at Nick and then back at Corey. "Okay?"

He nodded and threw his arms around Darcy. She held him while Corey wept quietly against her shoulder.

Nick's heart swelled with emotions—love and hope—that he'd thought had been extinguished in him. Maybe there would be a happy ending for Corey.

A few minutes later, as the child drew back, a soft rap at the door prompted Nick to say, "Come in."

Bea entered with Abby and John Garrett. "They wanted to walk with you to your wing. Dinner will be served shortly."

Corey rose and went with his houseparents.

Bea waited until he was gone before asking, "How did it go?"

"As well as could be expected." Darcy glanced at the director and Nick. "Besides Fletcher Phillips, who else is Corey's relative?"

"We'll have to investigate that. His dad was the only one listed on the paperwork. Fletcher's name wasn't even on it."

"I'd like to help you with that. I've handled cases like Corey's before."

Part of Nick wanted to say that he could fill in temporarily until a relative was found, but the phone rang and Bea answered it. The other part of him was relieved he hadn't voiced that out loud. Pausing in her conversation, Bea cupped the receiver. "This may take a while. We can talk later, but, Darcy, I'll accept your help."

Darcy stood and left with Nick. Outside Bea's office, she stopped. "I need to talk with you somewhere quiet."

"This sounds serious."

"It is. There's something I need to tell you."

Chapter Ten

This was the moment when Darcy had to tell Nick why she had come to Haven in the first place. She still didn't know if she wanted to tell Fletcher, but she would have to say something to her biological father because of her growing feelings for Corey. She could give him a mother's love.

Corey needed a home. She wanted to give him one. And from all she'd gathered concerning Fletcher, he wouldn't stand in the way. He'd be relieved he didn't have to do anything.

"Since everyone will be at dinner in a few minutes, I'm sure there'll be a spare room we can talk in." Nick led her down the hallway toward the front of the large house. He poked his head into a small room used for parent visits. "This is free."

Not sure where to start, Darcy turned to face

him while he shut the door. She'd come to really care for Nick, and it felt right to share her past with him. If only she knew more about him. She wished he wasn't such a private man. Regardless, she needed to tell him because of how much he cared for Corey.

"Let's sit." She waved her hand at the couch behind her. When she was settled and Nick sat next to her, she drew in a deep breath, held it for a few seconds and then released it. "I have wonderful parents who have loved me from the beginning. But Mom and Dad are my adoptive parents. I've known most of my life and it never made a difference. I'm their daughter in every sense except a biological one."

"I had a good friend who was adopted. He had a wonderful set of parents like you did."

"When I became sick last year and was diagnosed with celiac disease, which is hereditary, I wanted to know more about my biological parents. It's no secret I want a family and children, but what would my illness do to my kids? It's manageable, but what if there was some condition in my birth father's or mother's family that was even more serious? I needed to find that out."

His eyebrows scrunched together. "Why are you telling me this now?"

She rushed ahead and said, "Because Fletcher

Phillips is my birth father and therefore Corey is my cousin."

Nick's face wore a stunned expression, from his dropped jaw to his wide eyes glued to hers. Then he turned his head, and when he peered back at her, his features were composed into a neutral look, almost a bored one, as though she'd read him her grocery list. The silence lengthened into an uncomfortable sensation.

Finally she said, "Say something."

"What am I supposed to say? Congratulations?"

"Definitely not that. I'm not even sure I'm going to tell Fletcher, but then I probably will have to because I want to apply to be Corey's guardian."

"Why? You haven't known him long."

"I know he needs a family. I'm that. I know Fletcher won't take him in. Besides him, I'm probably one of Corey's closest family members."

Nick surged to his feet. "Well, it looks like you've got everything figured out."

"I thought this would be good news."

"Is Corey your new pet project? What if he doesn't want to go with you? This is his home. Not Alabama."

Ah, he was worried about Corey's reaction and the boy being states away. Any move could be hard on Corey—and Nick—but the child needed someone who wanted to care for him. "I'd stay until everything is worked out, but yes, I would move him to my home. My parents would accept him into our family as though he were my child. Corey needs a loving family."

"You're right. I hate to cut this short, but I've got chores still to do at my ranch. Good night, Darcy." He strode from the room so fast she didn't even have time to stand before he was gone.

Leaving her to wonder what was really going on.

Did he have hopes of raising Corey now that Ned was gone?

She started after Nick, but by the time she emerged from the house, he was driving away from the boys ranch. Should she go after him?

She'd left her purse in Bea's office. She hurried back to get it and go after Nick. Her bag in hand, she stepped into the hallway and ran into Corey.

"Are you leaving?" he asked in a quavering voice.

"I was, but if you want me to stay, I can."

He nodded and then looked down at his feet.

All she wanted to do was hug him and never let him go. She'd always wanted to be a wife and mother, like her own mom was, and had never thought of adopting, but this was right. She gathered him against her, and he clung to her.

Somehow she would have to tell Fletcher the truth before she applied for guardianship as Corey's relative. And somehow she would make Nick understand how she felt.

At the fund-raising meeting on Wednesday night, Nick sat across from Darcy. He'd done a good job of avoiding her. Flint was the one who had contacted her about the details of the rodeo on Saturday.

Until he'd had to face the threat of Corey leaving the area, Nick hadn't realized how much he'd come to love the child. He saw so much of himself in Corey that it was scary. The yearning. The need. The anger. Even now he couldn't let go of his deep hurt and rage at his father, feelings much like what Corey told Nick he was experiencing. But Nick also realized how wonderful Darcy would be as a mother to Corey. It would be perfect if she adopted Corey and stayed here. Then he could see the boy and continue helping him learn to ride and whatever else he needed. But Darcy had other plans.

As Darcy wrapped up the meeting, he leaned forward, ready to leave as soon as possible.

"I sent out a news release about the fund-raiser to the papers in the area," Darcy said. "Tomorrow Carol and Josie are going to blanket the surrounding towns with flyers. Thanks, Katie, for designing it and running off hundreds of copies for us. I'll see everyone early Saturday morning."

Nick hopped to his feet to go.

"Nick, could you stay a few minutes after the meeting? I have a couple of questions about the animals, and since Flint couldn't make it, I hope you can answer them."

As the committee members filed out of the room, he stood looking everywhere but at Darcy. She was Fletcher's daughter, and now she wanted to take Corey away from Haven, from him. He'd come close to telling her why Corey was so important to him. Now he was glad he hadn't revealed his relationship with his dad. He still didn't know what he'd done to deserve a father like his. He'd tried to do everything right, but nothing he had done had pleased his old man.

Suddenly Darcy was in front of him, only a couple of feet away. Concern lit her eyes, tempting him to beg her not to take Corey. To stay instead.

"I need a horse that I can do tricks on. I know this is last minute, but the more events we have in the rodeo the better it will be. I used to trick ride as a teenager and was part of the entertainment at horse shows."

Trick riding? He knew she had ridden, but that was a skill most riders didn't have. She'd been so open with him, or so he'd thought, but now he realized she had her own secrets. What else?

"I have a horse at the Flying Eagle that would be a good one to use. You could try Rose and see if you two are compatible. I noticed on the flyer that there was mention of a surprise. Is that it?"

"Yes. But if I don't do it, I'll come up with another surprise for the audience."

"When was the last time you did any tricks?" He could see similarities between Darcy and Fletcher. The same dark blond hair and blue eyes, even down to a cleft in their chins. Why hadn't he noticed it before?

"Four years ago at a fund-raiser. Not long after that my horse died, and I stopped doing it. We had a special bond." Her voice caught on that last sentence.

He started to reach for her but stopped. He needed to break ties, not make them deeper. As much as he cared for Corey and didn't want to see him go, he knew Darcy would make a great parent for the child—in Mobile. If only she wouldn't leave… "Is that all you want?"

"Yes, but—"

He turned to leave.

"I thought you would be happy that Corey

would have a home and not end up in the foster care system."

Don't answer her. Walk out the door.

"Are you mad at me?"

Darcy's question compelled Nick to stop and twist toward her. "Disappointed."

"I'm not Fletcher. I'm nothing like him."

"Are you so sure of that? You've been in Corey's life for a short time, and now you think you know what's best for him. You want to uproot him and take him away from the only place he's lived to be with strangers. Frankly he'd be better off at the boys ranch."

"He'll finally be taken care of and not left to fend for himself."

"Throwing money at him won't solve his problems. You told me you were a workaholic. Are you going to fall back into your usual pattern of working all the time? Corey doesn't need another parent who's never there."

She winced, thrusting her shoulders back. "I'll make time for him. I wouldn't take him on otherwise, and I'm not going to throw money at Corey. I'm going to love him."

"For how long? Until you marry and have your own children?" he asked before he could stop himself. She was great with the boys at the ranch, so why wouldn't she want to start a family of her own? But it was none of his business.

Darcy gasped. "If you could say that, then you don't know me. I'll check with Gabe and Tanner. Maybe they have a horse I can ride."

For the second time, he started toward the door.

"Nick, what's really going on? Do you want to take Corey? I'm not Fletcher, and I'd never treat Corey like Ned did."

No, I wouldn't be a good father for Corey, but I could be a friend. I can't, though, if he's in Mobile.

He continued his trek into the hallway and out the door to the parking lot. His pace slowed as he neared his truck. He didn't want her to have to look elsewhere for a horse she could use for trick riding. Rose would be perfect for her.

When he settled in the driver's seat, he took out his cell phone and texted her.

Come to the ranch tomorrow morning. My uncle will help you with Rose. I know you aren't Fletcher.

As he drove to the Flying Eagle, he kept telling himself Corey would have a family and that was all that mattered. But it didn't lift his spirits. He should be ecstatic for the child. He wasn't. The sadness of losing Corey overrode all other feelings.

When Nick entered his house by the back door, he hoped he could sneak to his bedroom and wallow in his grief. But Uncle Howard came into the kitchen before Nick could escape.

"Is there anything I need to know about the fund-raiser?" he asked as Nick passed.

"You and I are gonna help set up what we can on Friday afternoon. The rest will be done Saturday morning before the fund-raiser starts at twelve."

"Are you going to Ned's funeral at the gravesite in Dry Gulch tomorrow at one?"

"Yes, I told Bea I would take Corey. I don't imagine there will be many people there. I'm only going for Corey's sake."

"Maybe it's time you forgive your dad—and Ned. You should think about doing it tomorrow while you're saying your good-byes to Ned."

"He doesn't deserve forgiveness. Corey is alone in the world now, not that the man was much of a father to him when he was here."

"Who are you talking about? Your dad or Ned?"

"Both."

He stormed down the hallway and disappeared into his bedroom. All he wanted was to be left alone. But he couldn't rest. Instead, he paced the length of his room, fluctuating between anger at himself for how he'd handled losing Corey and anger at Darcy for coming into his life, turning it upside down and then planning to leave soon with a child he'd grown to care for—a child he loved.

Darcy finished loping around the corral, performing some of her tricks. She was a little rusty, but it was coming back—the technique and the fact that she missed riding on a horse even more than she'd realized when she rode with Corey and Nick. She dismounted and headed for the gate.

Howard opened it and clapped. "You have surprised this old coot. What made you start trick riding?"

"I saw a lady doing it when I was ten. She was great and so daring. It took a while before I could convince my parents I would be all right. Rose reminds me of the horse I had as a teenager." Darcy stroked the mare's neck.

When Rose turned and nudged her, Nick's uncle laughed. "She really likes you. And she doesn't cotton to everyone. But Nick has a knack of pairing a rider with the right horse."

"Where is Nick?"

"At the feed store."

"We didn't part on good terms last night."

"Yeah, he came home from the meeting as though he were a grizzly bear denied his sleep and yet he didn't get much last night. Did something happen at the church?"

"He knows that I'm going to apply to adopt Corey and, in the meantime, seek guardianship." Darcy walked the mare into the barn and removed the saddle.

Howard took it from her and returned it to where it belonged. "Now that's a surprise. Are you gonna move here?"

"No. My family and job are in Alabama."

"So you want to take Corey away. That explains why Nick has been so upset these past few days. Nick looks at Corey as if he is his younger brother. When Doug asked him to watch out for Corey and then was killed in the war, Nick took Doug's place in every sense. And Corey feels the same way about Nick. It might not be as easy as wanting to adopt the child. I know single people are able to adopt, but why do you think the state would give you guardianship?"

"Besides Nick, no one else in Haven knows this yet. That will change soon, but until I speak to Fletcher, please don't say anything to anyone but Nick."

"You want Fletcher to be your lawyer for the adoption?"

"No. I was adopted as a baby. Fletcher is my biological father, which makes Corey my cousin. When I first came to Haven, I didn't realize I had any family members here besides Fletcher. I'm going to tell Fletcher he's my birth parent and then use the fact that I'm Corey's cousin to apply for guardianship of him."

Howard rubbed the back of his neck, grabbed the reins and started for the exit. "I need to put her in the pasture. Walk with me." As they strolled out the door, he continued, "Now everything makes sense. Over the years Nick has been so reserved about his feelings and hasn't let many people close to him. Corey is one of the few he has, and honestly, when I've seen you two together, I see his walls breaking down."

"Why the walls?"

"I wish I could tell you, but it's Nick's story. All I can say is he didn't have an easy life from a young age." Howard opened the gate to a field and released Rose.

"Because of his father?"

Howard nodded.

"Did he go to the feed store because I was coming here?"

"Yes. I'm usually the one who does it. But he'll be coming home soon to get ready for Ned's funeral. He's taking Corey."

"Bea told me this morning. I hope he'll let me tag along. There's a chance of snow later, and I'd rather not drive. Do you think I should ask?"

"Yes, I see him returning from town. If you're gonna try to adopt Corey, you need to be with him as much as you can. Nick needs to learn to accept that and decide what's best for the child in the long term."

Nick parked near the opening to the barn, the back of his truck full of hay bales.

"I'll leave you to help him. I need to make a couple of calls." Howard winked and ambled away.

"Where's my uncle going?"

"To the house so we can talk."

Nick frowned and hefted the first hay bale. "We talked last night."

"I didn't mean to come in and take over with Corey. Until you told me about him, I didn't even know I had a cousin. Now that I do, it's hard for me to ignore it. I've always been a champion for projects involving children, so it was natural for me to gravitate toward the boys ranch."

Nick took another hay bale. "The reason Corey likes being with you is because you care about him. He can feel it."

Can you feel that I care about you too?

As Nick strode into the barn to put his load on a stack, Darcy grabbed one and struggled to lift it. But she did and made her way inside. "I'm telling you what I want, but if Corey is against it, I'll definitely take that into consideration. I wouldn't move him until he's visited my home." He skirted around her, and she hurried forward and stepped into his path, clasping his upper arms. "I haven't filed yet, and I won't until I tell Fletcher. I want Corey to realize I'm a relative and accept that first."

"You're leaving at the end of the month. That's a lot to get done in a couple of weeks. So why haven't you spoken to Fletcher?"

"Frankly, I'm not sure I even like the man, but then I don't know him well. I've only been around him a couple of times. And listening to you talk about him hasn't been encouraging that he would even acknowledge me."

"There's only one way to find out."

"I know. I thought after the fund-raiser was over I'd pay him a visit. Between looking for information about Avery Culpepper, volunteering at the boys ranch, spending time online working on a few ongoing cases and then organizing a fund-raiser in a short time, I didn't realize how stretched I was until I fell into bed last night, dead tired but unable to sleep. Too much was swirling around in my mind."

"Me too. I'm sorry about what I said yesterday. I know you have Corey's best interests at heart, and if you adopting him is good for him, then I won't stand in your way."

She held out her hand. "Still friends then?" Although, as she said *friends*, she realized she wanted more.

He took her hand, tugged her close and kissed

her forehead. "I can't stay mad at you. Would you like to go with Corey and me to Ned's funeral?"

"Yes. When?"

"I'm picking him up at school around twelve so we can be in Dry Gulch in time. We'll pick you up at 12:10 p.m. at the Blue Bonnet."

She gave him a grin. "See you then."

After the funeral in Dry Gulch, Nick drove his truck toward Haven with Corey sitting between Darcy and him. Snow fell, blanketing the landscape. He reduced his speed, but a lot of the snow wasn't sticking on the road, only on the grass.

Remembering how Darcy felt about driving in this kind of weather, Nick slanted a look at her. As Corey stared silently at the dashboard, lost in thought, she had her arm around the boy, giving him her quiet support as she had done throughout the funeral.

In that moment he knew that Darcy would be a great mother for Corey, and he couldn't stand in her way if the boy wanted her to adopt him. Nick realized he could help them bond. Maybe it was better that she became Corey's guardian. He'd said for years he didn't want to be responsible for a family. He'd seen and been in the middle of one that fell apart.

If only she would stay so he could see Corey grow up.

Darcy glanced at Nick. "I should be panicking now because the fund-raiser is in two days, but the weatherman said it will be well above freezing tomorrow and Saturday will be even warmer. Do you think the snow will melt by then?"

"Yes. This isn't going to stay around long. I predict by midmorning it'll start melting." Nick sent her a reassuring smile.

Blinking, Corey perked up and looked out the windshield. "I love snow."

"Where I live in south Alabama we don't get much at all, but this is the second snowfall I've seen since I came here."

"I like playing outside and making things in the snow. Snow sngels. Forts. Snowmen." Corey's voice became more excited as he talked.

"How about a snowwoman? I've never done either one."

Corey and Nick exchanged glances and then Corey whispered into his ear, "Can we make one with Darcy?"

Nick nodded. He would have to content himself with being a friend long-distance, but right now he would cherish every moment he could with Corey.

Corey twisted back to Darcy. "We'll show you how to build a snowman."

"And a snowwoman?" Darcy asked with a chuckle.

"Yup. And I've got a good idea," Nick added. "I'll call Miss Bea and tell her you're gonna stay for dinner at my place and then I'll bring you back to the boys ranch. Before we eat, we can make them in my front yard."

"What if it doesn't stop snowing?" Darcy asked.

"We can do it while it's snowing. You won't melt." Nick winked at her, feeling his cold heart beginning to thaw.

After drinking a cup of the hot chocolate that Howard had fixed for them, Darcy traipsed outside behind Nick and Corey, ready to build her snowwoman. "Okay, all I have to do is make a snowball and then roll it on the ground until it gets as big as I want?"

"Corey, I think she's got it. You did good explaining it to her." Nick held his hand up, and the boy high-fived him. "Now, are you sure you don't want me to help you make your snowman?"

Corey nodded. "Darcy will need your help."

She planted her fist on her waist. "I beg your pardon. I'm capable of doing this by myself."

Nick scanned the yard. "Tell you what. I think there's enough snow that we each can make one and let Uncle Howard decide which is the best."

"Y'all shouldn't even bother. I'm gonna beat you." Corey scooped up a handful of snow and packed it into a ball.

Darcy started hers. As she stooped over to roll it along the ground, a snowball struck her side. She shot straight up and whirled around. Nick bent over to make another while Corey took what he had in his hand and pelted her with it.

"I can't believe y'all are ganging up on me." Darcy launched her snowball at Nick.

Then suddenly Corey followed suit. The next ten minutes he teamed up with her. He probably felt sorry for her. But that was okay.

Nick ducked behind his truck and popped up to toss several balls quickly one after another, all at her.

She tried to dodge them but instead stumbled and went down. She was covered with snow, but so were Nick and Corey. Her laughter filled the air, her tears of joy streaking down her cold face. "I call a truce."

Nick brushed what snow he could off his coat. "I couldn't resist the chance."

Corey shook his head, loosening the white flakes. "Me neither. Do we still have time to make a snowman?"

Nick looked up at the darkening sky. "If we hurry and work together. Darcy, you make the head. I'll do the bottom and, Corey, you make the middle."

Darcy trudged across the yard. "I'll be over here away from you two. If I get any wetter, I'll freeze into an ice statue." She disappeared around the side of the house.

She wouldn't trade the past half an hour for anything. She quickly made her head ball and picked it up to carry back. But before she rounded the corner, she stopped and peeked into the front yard in case they had set up an ambush.

Instead, Corey was helping Nick roll a huge ball to a spot near the porch where a medium one was. When Corey set his middle ball on top of the base, he stepped back and grinned from ear to ear. "This is gonna be the best snowman."

Darcy glanced at her pitifully small head and hurriedly added more to it, packing it down as much as possible. She was not going to be the one to ruin their masterpiece.

"Darcy, do you need help?" Corey came around the side of the house.

"I was just coming back to put the finishing touch on the snowperson." She held up the head, not totally pleased with its size, but it was much better than it had been.

When she set it on the unfinished snowman,

she made a big production out of it, hoping no one would say anything about her attempt.

Nick was barely able to keep a straight face. Finally he turned his back on them—probably so she wouldn't see his grin.

"I know. Not the best in the world," she murmured and started to take it off the snowman.

Corey stopped her. "Don't. I think it's fine. Dontcha, Nick?"

Nick pivoted and, with a solemn expression, nodded, but his eyes twinkled.

To Darcy's relief, Howard stepped out on the porch. "I'm starving, so I decided to bring out a hat, scarf, carrot and chocolate pieces for the mouth and eyes. Corey and Nick, go get two branches while Darcy decorates the face."

"Thanks, Howard. I didn't know they wanted to make a giant snowperson."

"That's Texans for you. They like to do things big." Howard plopped the black cap on top of the snowman's head while Darcy stuck on the carrot and then the pieces of chocolate.

When Nick and Corey returned and planted the sticks in place, Howard pulled out his cell phone. "Okay, y'all stand by your work of art and smile."

Instead of grinning, Nick and Corey laughed, tried not to and couldn't stop.

Darcy watched them feed off each other. Nick

didn't want a family. That was such a shame. She'd always wanted one.

Finally, the guys settled down, and Howard took a photo. "I'll make sure everyone gets a picture. Now let's go eat."

As Corey entered the house with Howard, Nick hung back with Darcy. "Thanks for being a good sport. For a little while Corey was able to forget and just be a kid."

"I know. But he'll have to deal with his past and his mixed feelings concerning his dad."

"Yeah. Too bad they don't just go away on their own."

"Are you talking about your own father or Ned?"

"Both." He slung his arm over her shoulders and headed for the entrance.

But the fun of the past hour had evaporated. When would Nick trust her to tell her about his father?

Later when Nick drove toward the boys ranch to drop off Corey, he was tired. He stifled a yawn. Today had been an emotional day for the child and, for that matter, Nick too. He wanted to be part of Corey's life. He didn't want him to leave—or Darcy either, especially after the camaraderie they'd shared while playing in the snow. He thought he had everything worked out, but then his emotions fluctuated when reality set in and Darcy commented on Corey dealing with his father's death.

When they said good-night to Corey in the entry hall at the boys ranch, Corey gave him a hug and then so did Darcy, who also kissed the top of his head.

"We'll see you tomorrow. After school, we'll practice your barrel racing with the others." Nick tousled Corey's hair. "You're a natural at riding. If I didn't know better, I would think you've been riding for a while."

Corey beamed. As he mounted the stairs, he turned halfway up and waved at them.

When Nick slid into the driver's seat, he stared at the large ranch home. "I think today went well. Corey's gonna sleep well tonight." He wasn't sure *he* would though. If Darcy took Corey to Alabama, a part of him would go with them.

"I hope so. I could use a good night's sleep too. We have a lot to do in the next two days, even more if the snow remains. I love the open-house concept for the fund-raiser. My goal is to give Fletcher a tour of the ranch. I've sent him an invitation, and I intend to follow up on it tomorrow."

"Are you going to tell him who you are?" Nick started his truck.

"No. I need him to see the value of the ranch. I don't want to confuse the issue with that revelation."

"In other words, you're putting it off."

She chuckled. "Am I that obvious?"

"Yep, but I don't blame you."

"My preference is to never tell him, but I need to establish that Corey is a relative."

Curious about her reasons, he asked, "Why wouldn't you tell Fletcher?"

"Because I already have a dad, and frankly Fletcher isn't my idea of a father."

"What about the medical information you're seeking?" He threw her a glance as he approached Haven.

"After meeting him and seeing his stand on the boys ranch, I've been reconsidering it. I could get some of the medical information by digging deep into his family and talking to people who knew Luella Snowden Phillips. I'd love to find out all I can on her. From what I've learned she was quite a woman, who had a wonderful dream with the first boys ranch. Too bad Fletcher isn't more like his grandmother."

"Sometimes close relatives can be as different as night and day." His dad and Uncle Howard had been like that.

"True. I've seen enough of that in my job."

"Do you enjoy being a lawyer?"

"Yes. Many people need a good attorney but can't pay for one. I feel like I'm helping people who can't."

"You're definitely different from Fletcher in that respect. Too bad you can't stick around and maybe become a good influence on Fletcher."

As Nick pulled up to the Blue Bonnet Inn, she asked, "I don't know that who I am would influence him one way or another. He seems pretty set in his ways."

"Yeah, you're right. I've been trying for sixteen months to get him to do something about Ned." When Darcy pushed down on the handle, he added, "I'll walk you to the porch."

"You don't have to."

"I want to." He hurried and rounded the hood as she hopped down from the cab.

A light illuminated the porch, highlighting her beautiful features. Her eyes, a glittering blue, weren't really like Fletcher's. There was a shine in them that drew Nick every time he looked at her. And her luxurious blond hair, long and wavy, framed her face and emphasized her attributes—not just outward but inward too.

Nick turned toward Darcy. "I was dreading the funeral and how Corey would do. I'm glad we went together."

"So am I. If I drove, I'd probably be stuck

somewhere between Dry Gulch and Haven. I felt you lose control of your truck a few times."

"I'm surprised you didn't say anything."

"No reason. You knew what you were doing." She sighed. "I don't know if it's really hit Corey yet that his father is gone. But the houseparents and Bea are sharp and will be quick to pick up on anything wrong."

"And let us know if we need to help."

"Yes, exactly."

Darcy had made Corey's transition to the boys ranch so much easier. She'd become so important to Nick. There were times he floundered with what to do or say, but Darcy knew the perfect thing.

Darcy moved closer to Nick, and he held his ground, enjoying her nearness. "Don't fall asleep driving home."

"I won't."

"Maybe you could call me and let me know you got to your ranch all right." She ran her palm down his jawline, her eyelids closing partway.

That was all the invitation he needed. His arms encircled her, bringing her tight against him as he dipped his head and took her mouth in a kiss.

He wanted it to last, but the sound of a car door slamming nearby parted them as they shifted to see who was coming toward the house. Avery. And Fletcher was parked behind Nick's truck.

"See you tomorrow." He gave her hand a gentle squeeze and headed for his pickup whistling, his gaze on Fletcher's glare.

"My, my. It looks like you had an interesting date," Avery said as she stopped next to Darcy.

"How about you?" Darcy curled her hands at her side, trying to remember that she still wanted to get some more information from the brash woman, who was dressed in four-inch heels and a tight skirt that stopped three inches above her knees.

Avery waved her hand in the air. "Just business."

Darcy entered the bed-and-breakfast with Avery right behind her. "Maybe you can help me. On Saturday, when the boys ranch will be open to the public for tours, I wanted to give background information about the Culpepper family, who so generously donated the land and house. What was your father's name?"

"John."

"Your mother's name?"

Avery continued toward the staircase, forcing Darcy to hurry to keep up. "Mommy is all I remember."

"Isn't it on your birth certificate?"

"I'm sure it would be if I had one. Now, if you'll excuse me, I'm tired and want to go to bed." Avery practically ran up the stairs and disappeared from view.

Darcy sank onto a step. The woman knew her father's name because it was in the will but didn't know who her mother was. Avery was definitely an impostor. She really had nothing to back up her claims.

Darcy would talk with Lana and Bea after the fund-raiser was over. Something needed to be done quickly because time was running out for fulfilling the terms of Cyrus Culpepper's will.

Chapter Eleven

Nick stood at the entrance the participants were using for the boys ranch's First Annual Rodeo for Youths. The bleachers that Pastor Andrew had borrowed for the fund-raiser lined the inside of the riding arena. Flint was at the other end of the ring, making sure everything ran smoothly, and so far it had.

Hundreds of people from Haven and the surrounding towns had come out to watch the boys participate in barrel racing, team penning and showmanship. Corey was in the beginner group for barrel racing. He would be the last to perform.

"Has Corey raced yet?" Darcy asked from behind Nick.

He glanced over his shoulder and saw her holding the reins to Rose. "Nope. He's coming up now."

Darcy gave Corey a thumbs-up while Nick

opened the gate and patted Rose's flank. Corey entered the arena to the cheers of the crowd. He grinned from ear to ear. Wyatt was the starter for each event, but he was also there in case there was a medical problem with one of the animals. Dr. Delgado was nearby if a boy was hurt.

Wyatt dropped his arm, indicating the start, and Corey shot forward, racing toward the red, white and blue barrel at the far end. He slowed to round it and then picked up speed to cross the finish line near Nick.

"He did good," Darcy said beside Nick.

"Yeah, but he was two seconds behind the winner."

"Enough for second place."

"Yep," he said as the first three places were announced over the loudspeaker.

Darcy shouted "Hurrah!" for each winner but louder for Corey. The biggest grin shone bright on the kid's face. "Now it's my turn. I hope I don't mess up. The boys will never let me live that down."

"If they give you any grief, challenge them to do the trick. On second thought, don't. Without training, they'd break their necks."

"Safety while riding is important. I should know—I've broken my arm and leg over the years."

"And that didn't discourage you?"

"No. It made me more determined. Both times it was because I was pushing myself beyond what I or my mount was ready to do."

Gabe Everett, the emcee for the rodeo, took the mic. "We wanted to end this with a special act from Darcy Hill, who has performed tricks on a horse countless times at various shows in the South. Let's give her a big Texas welcome."

Thunderous clapping and feet stomping resonated through the riding arena. Darcy's cheeks reddened as she swung up into her special saddle, which she'd had her father ship overnight, along with the hot-pink, sequined outfit she wore.

While Rose galloped around the ring, Darcy started off swinging out of the saddle, touching the ground and then landing in front of the horn, facing backward. She did several dismounts and then performed a reverse neck and a spritz layout. The crowd roared. She ended with a hippodrome like the Romans did thousands of years ago, where she stood up and made a complete circle around the arena, waving to the audience.

Nick didn't realize he had been holding his breath through the last trick, but finally he inhaled deeply. To a standing ovation, Darcy came to a stop in the center, dismounted and then bowed to each side. Several boys, including

Corey, ran to her, pumping their arms in the air. They encircled her, all asking questions at once.

As more boys gathered around Darcy, Nick hurried to rescue Rose from the onslaught. His mare was gentle and used to people but not a crowd. When he reached the circle of children, he noticed how calm Rose was, even when the kids got close to check the special saddle. Darcy showed them the extra straps on it, fielding one question after another.

"Can I learn how?" Corey asked and then more kids chimed in.

"It takes a lot of practice to do these tricks. You have to be an accomplished rider and have the right horse." Darcy looked at Nick over the sea of kids from the ranch and town. "But more than anything, don't do these tricks without an adult. I had an uncle who taught me when I was ready."

Nick watched Darcy interacting with the children. She was patient and made sure everyone had her full attention. In that moment he knew Corey would be fine with Darcy as his guardian—even if they both lived in Alabama. But would he?

That question took him by surprise. He loved Corey, but he was willing to let him go if it was better for him. He was struggling to make his ranch a thriving business once more. That should be where his focus was. Darcy was doing him a favor.

Yeah, right. Then why don't you believe that?

As the throng of kids dissipated to get samples of the food being offered outside in the tents, Corey remained next to Darcy.

He pointed at Rose. "Can I ride her out of the ring?"

She smiled at Corey and gave him a leg up. As he sat tall in the saddle, Fletcher approached Darcy.

Darcy spied Nick coming around the other side of Rose while she kept her attention on the man who was her birth father. "I'm glad to see you at the fund-raiser." Hope flared in her that this would lead to Fletcher changing his mind about the boys ranch.

"Well, yes, but I'm not going to stay. My secretary gave me your note and the ticket to this… event." The attorney handed Darcy a ten-dollar bill. "I appreciate the gesture of free admission, but I can pay my own way."

"Darcy, I'll take Rose and Corey out of here."

She peered at Nick, wishing he could stay but realizing she had to do this alone. "Thank you. I'll come to the barn later to get my saddle."

As Nick and Corey left with the mare, Darcy turned back to Fletcher. "I understand how you may feel about the boys ranch being moved from your family's place, where it all started. Your grandmother sounds like a forward-thinking woman who cared about the community. It was a tribute to her."

He opened his mouth to say something.

Darcy hurriedly continued, "The boys ranch will always be her idea. Even though they have expanded and moved here, she will always be the founder of the Lone Star Cowboy League Boys Ranch. You must be really proud of Luella Snowden Phillips and the good she has accomplished."

"You've been in town two weeks. I'm sure by now, especially since you're friends with Nick McGarrett, you know I'm not a fan of the boys ranch."

Darcy gritted her teeth as he spoke and then forced a smile on her face. "Have you had a tour of the place?"

"No, don't see why I should. I knew what the original one was like and I didn't like the idea of a boys ranch even then."

"Before you pass judgment, don't you think you should see it all? That way, you'll be talking from a place of knowledge." Her grin wavered as Fletcher scowled. She shored it up and finished with, "Let me show you what the boys ranch is about and then you can say you're completely informed."

"I don't have much time."

She hooked her arm through his and walked toward the exit. "Then let's get started. We'll begin with the house and the three wings where the boys live with a couple in each wing who are the houseparents for them."

As they strolled toward the ranch house, Fletcher scanned the food tents, craft tables and games for the crowd. "You're not from around here. What made you come to Haven?"

"A vacation."

His bushy eyebrows slashed downward. "Haven has never been a vacation spot. I'd think you'd go skiing in the mountains or lie on a beach somewhere."

"I live near a beach and I don't ski." Darcy wanted to tell Fletcher he was the reason that she was here, but this wasn't the right time. Today was about the boys ranch. She entered the house through the front door. "I've only been here a short time, and I've seen what this place can do for a boy who needs help."

"Isn't that what a detention center for juvenile delinquents is for?"

"The boys ranch takes children from age six to seventeen. A young child isn't a juvenile delinquent. So many need guidance and time to develop their social and emotional skills." Darcy led Fletcher through one of the wings. "Take, for example, Corey, who is the most recent boy to come here. In less than two weeks, he has improved his reading, taken care of a horse and learned to ride. He's become a valuable team player. They all have chores that they're responsible for and those rotate, so they have a lot of experience in different areas."

"Isn't that what a parent is for?" Fletcher asked as they walked to one of the other wings.

The thought that he was her biological father and had just asked that irritated her. Where was Fletcher when she was born? "Ideally, yes, but life doesn't work out that way all the time. Corey lost his dad recently, but before that he'd run away from his house because his father was drinking too much and not taking care of him."

Pressing his lips together, Fletcher glared at her. He slowed his pace.

She probably shouldn't have said that. She had let her feelings toward Fletcher get the better of her. She smiled. "In Corey's case, like so many others, there isn't a good alternative. Some come here because they need social skills or they have to learn to manage their behavior, but above all else, this is a safe environment for the children. There are no boys with psychotic disorders. That's not what this facility is for."

"You could have fooled me. One of them is most likely responsible for burning the barn down."

Stopping in her tracks, she cocked her head and asked, "Do you realize that many people in town think *you* are behind the fire?"

His eyes grew round. "Me! I'd never do something like that. I'll stop this place legally, not illegally."

Darcy strolled through the kitchen to the back door. "Let me show you the old barn, where some of the livestock is kept. There are goats, sheep, cattle and horses."

"I've seen a barn before." He pointed to the building nearby. "What's that?"

"That's the library, where the children get help with their school work. I've been tutoring them after school since I arrived. I love seeing a child's expression when he finally understands something. Not far away are the basketball and volleyball courts. Exercising in fun ways helps promote healthy growth."

"It looks like a country club to me."

Anger burst from its restraints. "And what is wrong with that? They help take care of the house and ranch. They learn responsibility and develop a good self-image that will help them become productive citizens. You were fortunate to have been born into wealth. Most are not."

"I've worked hard for what I have."

"So what do you think we should do with these twenty-four boys? Give them what they need to become good citizens or let them loose with no support and possibly lead them down the path of juvenile delinquents? Wasn't your father and his behavior the reason your grandmother started the ranch?"

Fletcher harrumphed. "That was different."

"How?"

"I—I…" He tipped his Stetson and finally said, "Good day, Ms. Hill."

As the man stormed off, she sat down on the back steps. She'd made this worse. She'd hoped showing him the ranch and the good it did would change his mind. She'd been wrong. She prayed the boys didn't pay for her mistake.

Leaving the staff and the boys to clean up after the fund-raiser, Nick strolled to his truck, intending to help set up for the ladies' choice dance and then go home. It had been a long day. When he started to climb into the cab, he stopped in midmotion.

He stepped back out and picked up the envelope lying on his seat. His name was scrawled across the front in blue ink. He opened the letter and pulled it out.

The note read, *Wanna go to the dance tonight with me? Pick me up at 8. Love, Darcy.*

For a few seconds, he stared at the word *love* and imagined them as a couple. Then his gaze slid to the first word.

Wanna? He hadn't seen Darcy's handwriting, but he was sure she didn't write this. Then he remembered what some of the others had received over the past months, and he chuckled. Someone was playing matchmaker.

He looked up and panned the yard for anyone watching. If they were, they were hiding well.

But, to be on the safe side, he needed to check with Darcy. She didn't deserve to be stood up. Darcy was on the set-up committee so she would be at the church. He hopped into his truck and drove there, trying to figure out how he would ask her about the note.

When he arrived at the reception hall where the dance would take place, he glanced around for Darcy. Her car was in the parking lot. He spied her standing on a tall ladder putting up one end of the banner while Lana tacked up the other part.

"Is that even?" Darcy asked as she leaned back to decide.

"It's even," he called out.

The ladder wobbled. Nick hurried to her in case she fell. But she immediately flattened herself against the ladder and grasped it. It wavered and then settled into place.

Slowly she descended. When she turned, he glimpsed a pink tinge across her cheeks. "I'll be the first one to tell you I know what a hammer is, but I can be lethal when I use it. This time I only hit my thumb once."

"You should have waited."

"I thought you might get stuck at the ranch dealing with the animals."

"Nope. Flint and some of the older boys were finishing up at the barn and suggested I come see if you need any help."

She pushed the hammer into his hand. "Here. Any hammering can be done by you."

He chuckled. "I didn't get to ask you about the tour you gave Fletcher."

"A disaster."

"Did you tell him who you were?"

"No, definitely not the right time."

Nick pulled the note from his back pocket. "I found this in my truck on the seat. Did you send it?"

She retrieved one exactly like his, except the wording was different. "Obviously you didn't send this."

"Nope. It's a ladies' choice dance."

She blushed. "Up until recently things were tense between us, and then today was so crazy.

I'm glad I remembered to come here to set up. Nick, would you like to go to the dance with me tonight?"

He grinned. "We shouldn't encourage the matchmaker, but since it could be Corey, I wouldn't want to disappoint him. As the note says, I'll pick you up at eight."

"Which only gives us a couple of hours to decorate and get home to change."

"Yep, so what do you want me to do?"

"Help me set up the tables and chairs first. I should be okay. No hammer involved."

As they walked to the closet where the tables were stored, his earlier exhaustion seemed to lift. There was a spring to his step. Darcy brightened his day and that scared him. What was he going to do when she left Haven?

"Did you hear what happened with Pastor Andrew?" Nick asked, hoping to take Darcy's mind off dancing.

"Yes, Katie told me earlier that he showed up to pick her up for the dance. Apparently the same matchmaker left him a note in his car at the fund-raiser, but Katie didn't get one. She told me when she saw him she was speechless."

"I saw them arrive together. Pastor Andrew didn't know what else to do."

Darcy moved closer to Nick. "As Katie was telling me, she was turning ten shades of red."

When Bea joined them, she was using a paper plate as a fan. "Is it just me or is it hot in here?"

"It's comfortable to me, but then I haven't been dancing like you have," Darcy said.

"That's because all these single men have been coming up to me and telling me I asked them to the dance. They received a note to meet me here at the church."

"Who?" Nick could barely contain his laughter.

"Seth Jacobs, the grocer and Slim. I've been shuffling between them. I don't want to hurt their feelings and tell them I didn't leave a note for them. I think I'll lose five pounds tonight if this keeps up." Bea's eyes grew wide as a deputy sheriff headed toward her. "Oh, no. Not another one. See you two later. I'm ducking into the restroom." Bea scurried away in the opposite direction of the officer.

Darcy looked at Nick and chuckled. "Poor Bea. Whoever the matchmakers are, they have been busy today."

Nick grinned. "I guess they really wanted Bea to dance tonight. I don't dance. I'm glad it was her, not me."

"Speaking about dancing, shouldn't we?" she asked as one song ended and another started.

"Ah, finally a slow dance," Nick said, holding out his hand to Darcy.

She placed hers in his. "Remind me to teach you a Texas line dance in our spare time."

He laughed. "When will that be?"

"After tonight, I'll be a gal on vacation. So you can fit me into your busy schedule."

His arms wrapped around her, and he moved in close, her light fragrance flirting with his senses. The music and people surrounded them, but all Nick focused on was Darcy in his embrace. Her soft hair grazed the side of his face, and suddenly he wished they weren't in the middle of a crowded dance floor.

He attempted to shove that thought out of his mind. She wanted a family. He wasn't cut out to be a father. What if he failed like his dad? He'd finally acknowledged that when she had stated she wanted to adopt Corey. If only the boy could stay here in Haven so he could be part of his life without being a father figure. When he'd been looking out for Corey, he'd considered himself to be taking Doug's place. A big brother he could do.

Lost in thought, he stepped on Darcy's foot. She hardly missed a beat and didn't say a word. "Sorry about that."

She leaned back and looked up into his face. "You warned me. Actually you're doing fine."

"You're kind to say that, but I saw you wince."

The music wound down, and some of the couples left the floor. When a fast tune blared from the loudspeakers, he grabbed her and tugged her toward the sidelines.

She limped.

"Is your toe broken?"

She laughed and adjusted her gait. "No, but I love teasing you."

He drew her into a dimly lit corner and caged her against the wall. "You're brave, teasing me—and dancing with me."

"All you need are a few lessons. Maybe I can add slow dancing to the Texas line dancing lessons before I leave."

He tensed. "When is that happening?"

"I've started the proceedings to adopt Corey so it might be a while. I'm trying to prove my relationship to him without including Fletcher."

"You aren't going to tell him?"

"After what happened today at the ranch, I don't know that I'm ever going to tell him he's my biological father."

Someone gasped close by.

Darcy looked around Nick and glimpsed Avery a few feet away, almost concealed by a pocket of darkness.

Chapter Twelve

Before Darcy could say anything, Avery scurried from her hidden spot and out into the crowd of dancers, weaving her way through them.

As Nick moved, Darcy moaned. "Avery overheard what I said. Leave it to her to be sneaking around."

"She might not say anything to Fletcher," Nick said as he twisted around to face the partygoers.

Fletcher made a beeline for Darcy. "On second thought, she might. I don't want a scene in here. Let's leave the reception hall." Being close to one of the exits, she hurried for it, not prepared to see Fletcher. His attitude during the tour still bothered her. What had made him so judgmental—and mean?

Out in the foyer, Fletcher caught up with Darcy. Avery followed a few paces behind him.

"We need to talk before rumors start flying

around town," her birth father said in a tone that meant she didn't have a choice.

"Not here." Surprisingly, Darcy remained calm while Nick intercepted Avery and *escorted* her to the reception hall.

"Yes, here!" The fury in Fletcher's voice singed Darcy.

"Let's go into a classroom where the whole town won't hear." Darcy started walking toward the hallway off the foyer. At the door, she glanced over her shoulder at Fletcher.

He scanned the large entryway and several people leaving while a couple stood off to the side, watching him. He stormed after Darcy.

When Fletcher stepped into the room, he glared at Darcy. "You are *not* my daughter. I've never had a child. If you spread false rumors about me, I will sue you. What is your plan? To wheedle your way into my life to get my money?"

Remain calm. Anger won't make your point. "I don't need your money, and I don't want it. My father is Warren Hill, and he comes from a long line of wealth. He has a penthouse in New York City, a home in Hawaii and an estate in Alabama. Perhaps you've heard of him. He's a renowned attorney." She would not let him put down her *real* parents.

Fletcher didn't back down but moved closer.

"Then why are you spreading false rumors? Is it because I'm against the boys ranch?"

She placed a hand on her waist. "Why are you really against the boys ranch? In all the years it has been operating, Haven has grown. I don't see its existence as a deterrent to the growth of the town or the value of property here. You want to take away hope and a real chance for these boys to do better. Why are you so bitter?"

Fletcher's face flushed red. "I'm not bitter. I'm trying to save the town."

"And I'm not gullible. I don't buy that. Are you in with Avery, trying to milk as much money from the Culpepper estate as she can? Is that why you are representing a fraud?"

"Avery isn't a fraud! You are, if you think I'm buying this story of yours."

"You don't have to. I know what the truth is. You had an affair with Charlotte Myers and the result of that was me." She pointed at herself. "I have the birth certificate to prove it. Does Avery have one to prove who she is?"

His eyes narrowed, as if he were assessing Darcy and finding her lacking.

She didn't care what he thought. Charlotte had rejected her, so she really wasn't surprised that he would too. "I'm leaving. Frankly I wasn't going to say a word to you. All I wanted to do was find out about you and your family. To see if there were any heredity concerns I needed to be aware of. I love my parents who adopted me. I don't need you." She charged toward the hallway, needing to get away from her biological father.

As she left the classroom, she ran into Nick waiting for her. "I have to get out of here."

Nick put his arm around her shoulder and began walking in the direction of the exit. "I'll let Lana and Flint know we're leaving."

After he assisted Darcy into the passenger side of his truck, he made a call on his cell. At the moment she didn't want to be around others. A steamroller might as well have flattened her. She'd known her birth father would deny her. He hadn't really sought the truth, or he would have seen through the fake Avery.

As Nick started his pickup, he snuck a look at her. "Where do you want me to take you?"

"Home to Alabama." She said the first thing that came to her mind. She sighed. "But that isn't possible right now. I'm not going to let Fletcher get in my way. Please take me to the Blue Bonnet Inn. Everyone is at the dance, so I won't have to answer any questions."

When they reached the bed-and-breakfast, Darcy intended to say good-night then hole up in her bedroom to nurse her bruised feelings. But Nick opened the front door and entered before her as if he'd known what she was going to do.

"I'm not good company right now."

"That's okay. You don't have to talk, but if you do, I'm a good listener." He took her hand, drew her into the living room and sat next to her on the couch. "For as long as I've known Fletcher, he hasn't been a happy person. Where you look for the good in people, he looks for the worst."

"Why? What happened?"

"Maybe nothing. That might be what he's like."

Like Nick being so closed off. Had he always been that way? She didn't think so, but he didn't share himself with her.

"I think there's more. My biological mother wouldn't even talk to me. She had a family and wanted nothing to do with me."

Nick slipped his arm around her shoulders. "That's her loss. You're special, and she'll never find that out."

His words washed over her, numbing some of the hurt caused by the mother who gave birth to her. She'd hoped Fletcher wouldn't reject her too. "I need to look at my blessings in all of this. I have two terrific parents who loved me as though I was their biological daughter."

"See what I mean? You're already turning it around and focusing on the good. That doesn't come naturally for a lot of people." He stared across the room, a far-off look in his eyes.

He was referring to himself. She wished she could help him, but she'd asked him about his past and he'd avoided it. Telling her required trust, and he didn't trust easily.

"I try to keep my focus on the Lord," Darcy said. "When I do, it helps me get through the hard times."

"What if He's forgotten you?"

"He doesn't forget anyone. That doesn't always mean that your life will go smoothly, but He's beside you through those tough situations. You have to choose to take His support."

"So what are you going to do next concerning Fletcher?"

"Nothing. I'm still applying for guardianship of Corey. If Fletcher chooses not to believe me, that's his problem. He was listed on my original birth certificate. My main concern is for Corey. He does have family who cares."

"When are you going to tell Corey?"

"Probably Monday when I work with him. I want him to know now that I have the process for adopting him in the works. Are you okay about this? I know we've talked about this but—"

He placed his forefinger against her lips to still the rest of her sentence. "I don't want to lose Corey. He's become important to me, but once I stopped and thought about it, I realized you are the best person to take care of him."

He shifted closer to her and combed her hair back behind her ears, and then he cradled her head. As he slowly leaned toward her, she knew he was giving her time to pull away, but that was the last thing she wanted to do.

His mouth covered hers in a kiss that stole her heart. Nick had made coming to Haven so much easier than it could have been. She surrendered to the touch of his lips.

When he finally pulled back, his gaze caressed her face as though he were memorizing her features to remember later. "I figure Carol and Clarence will be coming home soon, so I'll leave and let you go upstairs. I know Carol. She'll quiz you on the dance the first chance she gets."

"And it's hard to keep from telling her everything. At least now I can freely tell her that Fletcher is my father if I want."

He rose and offered his hand to her. She took it, and he pulled her to her feet. He didn't release his grasp until he reached the front door and opened it. After a quick kiss good-bye, he left.

Her hand on the handle, she rested the top of her head against the door. She wanted more from him, but something was eating at him and he didn't trust her enough to share it with her.

He might not be capable or ready to do that. He'd quickly become important to her, but he didn't seem to return those feelings. She wanted a family. He didn't. It was that simple. Somehow she needed to start protecting herself from being crushed when she returned to her home in Alabama.

With a long sigh, Darcy headed for the staircase. The sound of someone inserting a key into the lock prodded her to go faster. But the door swung open when she put her foot on the second step. She glanced back and groaned.

"I need to talk to you." Avery's voice held a shriek to it.

"I'm tired and going to bed." Darcy continued up the stairs.

But Avery flew across the foyer and grabbed her arm, halting Darcy's escape. "I heard what you said about me being an imposter. How dare you accuse me of that. My grandfather died, and I get attacked."

Darcy shook off her hand and faced the woman, who was dressed in a rhinestone-and-sequined dress—Avery's attempt to appear as though she grew up on a ranch. It didn't work. "Do you mean, why did I state the truth?"

Carol and Clarence entered their house through the open door.

"What you said isn't true. Everyone knows it!" Avery yelled.

"Why? Because you said so? Do you have any real evidence to support that claim? Where is your birth certificate?"

"I don't have one. I was in foster care."

"I'm adopted and I have my original birth certificate. It hasn't been amended. I had to ask for it. Foster children have theirs and don't have to petition for it." In case Avery went to Fletcher, Darcy decided to add, "I know the names of my biological mother and father."

Avery's eyes became pinpoints, her forehead creased. She opened and closed her mouth, but no words came out.

"You had no idea your birth mother's name was Elizabeth and the real Avery was born on February 2."

Avery stiffened. "I knew that."

"No, you didn't. I asked those questions specifically."

The woman perched on the step below Darcy and stabbed her in the chest with her finger. "You're a liar."

"Like I said, come up with hard evidence to prove your claim or leave Haven now before I take this to the police. Come Monday morning I will. You knew facts that were easy enough to dig up if you did a search on Cyrus and John Culpepper on the internet or hired a private investigator."

Avery glared a hole through her as she shoved Darcy to one side and stormed up the staircase. When a bedroom door slammed closed, Carol and Clarence clapped.

"Thank you, Darcy. Information about your confrontation with Avery and Fletcher zoomed around the dance so fast I was getting whiplash."

"Everyone knows about Fletcher being my father?"

"By now, even the ones who didn't come tonight probably know."

"Good night, Carol, Clarence. I need some sleep." Hoping she could actually get some rest after everything that had happened, Darcy climbed the rest of the steps.

She didn't care if the news concerning Avery was fuel for the gossipers, but she hadn't wanted the fact that Fletcher was her father making the rounds. If only Avery hadn't overheard her and Nick talking, she could have picked the time and place. No doubt Fletcher would hunt her down again and let her know how upset he was that everyone in town knew that he had a child out of wedlock.

When Nick thought about kissing Darcy Saturday night, all he wanted to do was berate himself. She'd made it clear on a number of occasions that she would return to Alabama when Corey's adoption went through. The first time he saw her, she had *city gal* stamped all over her, and that hadn't changed in the few weeks she'd been here.

He'd fought hard these past sixteen months to make his family ranch a success again, and he was starting to see progress. Haven was in his blood. Ranching was his life. Being a father wasn't. He knew Darcy was disappointed in him for not sharing his past. He wanted to forget it, not dredge it up all the time. He'd wanted to please his father so much that every time he had rejected Nick, something died in him. He'd stopped hoping and didn't know how to get that hope back.

No, he was best as a bachelor like Uncle Howard. He'd failed as a son. Being a husband and father was much more difficult.

Wyatt finished examining Sunshine, a mare not in foal but one of the favorite horses at the boys ranch. "She's impacted. I'll give her something for it that should take care of the problem, but if it doesn't, let me know. Keep her in a stall and keep an eye on her progress."

Nick nodded. "Flint went into town. I'll tell him when he comes back here."

"I'll let you know when I'm finished treating her. Tell Johnny he did good picking up on something being wrong with Sunshine. It's much better when we catch it early."

"I will." Nick backed out of the stall and had turned to make his way to the tack room when he caught Gabe Everett coming into the barn. He headed toward the president of the Lone Star Cowboy League. "What's going on? Why the frown?"

"I came to let you and Flint know we're having an emergency meeting at my ranch tonight concerning Avery. Could you tell Flint I'd like Lana there? And could you ask Darcy to come too? After what happened Saturday, we need to make a decision concerning the woman who says she's Avery. If we don't accept her claim she is Avery, then we need to find the real one."

"I'll be there. Don't know about Darcy."

"I tried her at the Blue Bonnet Inn, but she wasn't there. It's important she comes. I figured you can persuade her."

"Sure." He didn't know if he could persuade her to do anything, especially keeping Corey here.

"We'll also talk about where we stand in finding the people in Cyrus's will. I'm afraid even if we have the right Avery, I'm the one who'll let everyone down. Tanner tried to find my grandfather and couldn't. I've tried too, but he seems to have vanished." Gabe swept his arm across his body. "All of this will be for nothing. We'll have to move back to the original ranch and only serve half the boys."

"I can't imagine what that would do to the boys. For so many of them, this is the chance they needed to make something of themselves." Nick stepped outside the barn. "I have to go home, but I'll track Darcy down if I need to."

Relieved, Gabe followed him to their trucks, which were parked side by side. "I'll leave a message on Flint's phone, but if you see him, let him know."

"I'll be back later."

"Good. I'm heading to the main house to meet with Bea. We need to start thinking about what our options are if we can't fulfill the will."

As Gabe strolled away, Nick climbed into his pickup and blew out a long breath. So much for staying away from Darcy.

Darcy stood on Fletcher's porch, poised in front of the door. She curled and uncurled her hands. Part of her wanted to hear why he had asked her to come to his house. Then she remembered Saturday night, and all she wanted to do was get in her car and return to Mobile. But she couldn't leave without Corey. She hadn't even told him yet she wanted to adopt him. What if he didn't want to be part of her family?

All yesterday that one question had plagued her. She wanted to talk to Nick about it, but he never returned her call. That was for the best. She was falling in love with him and couldn't see him living anywhere else but on his ranch and in Haven.

The front door swung open. Fletcher stood in the entrance, his solemn expression slowly vanishing to be replaced with a small smile. "I'm glad you came. I wasn't sure you would, but we need to talk and I don't think we should do it where others could overhear. Yesterday at church there were enough people talking about us. Come in."

Darcy hesitated, her teeth digging into her bottom lip. Should she risk another confrontation just because she was curious about what he wanted to say?

"Please, Darcy." He moved to the side to allow her into his house.

Without a word, she entered, not surprised by the massive mahogany table in the middle of the foyer, which displayed a vase of fresh flowers in the middle of winter. The hardwood floor held a high sheen with an expensive-looking woven rug under the table—more a piece of art than carpet.

"Let's go in here." He gestured to the left.

The rich ambiance of the entry hall spilled over into his large living room. The focal point was the huge marble fireplace with a few bronze Remington statues and a painting of an older woman above the mantle. "Who is that?"

"Luella Snowden Phillips. Would you like something to drink?" Fletcher asked so politely, his behavior different from how he'd acted the other day.

"No, I can't stay long. I tutor at the boys ranch after school."

He sat at the opposite end of the ivory-colored couch. This whole house shouted, "No children allowed."

He crossed one leg and reclined as though he had not a care in the world. "I've spent a lot of time thinking about our conversation the other night."

"So have I," she bit out, wishing she hadn't said anything. She didn't want to care, but she did.

"When I found out who you were, I was stunned. I said some things I shouldn't have. I had a knee-jerk reaction to a piece of big news I never thought I would hear. But when I got over the initial shock, I realized you could be my daughter. I did some checking. You're twenty-seven, and twenty-eight years ago I was in love with Charlotte." He looked away and swallowed several times. "I'd wanted to marry her and have a whole house full of children. She was everything to me, but then one day she disappeared, leaving me a note telling me not to look for her. She broke my heart."

As she did mine, Darcy thought. She and Fletcher had something in common besides family.

"I never let myself fall in love again. I hated the helplessness. I couldn't do anything to change the situation. I'd bought an engagement ring and was going to ask her to marry me that weekend. I never got the chance."

Loneliness dripped off each word, and Darcy hurt for him. She tried not to. There were so many reasons to be angry with him, but she couldn't.

"I never knew she was with child and that she gave birth to you. You have my coloring, but the shape of your mouth and nose is just like hers."

Darcy slipped her hand into the side pocket of her purse and removed her birth certificate. "In Alabama, I got my original one that listed my biological parents." She placed it on the couch between them.

He glanced at it and then lifted his gaze to hers. "I've been used to people trying to get something from me, and when you first told me, that was my reaction. But you don't need my money. Your adopted family is wealthier than I am. You've stated how much you love your adopted parents, so why did you come looking for me?"

"When I was diagnosed with celiac disease last year, I decided to search for my birth parents. Celiac is hereditary, and I wanted to know what else might be a problem in the future. I've always wanted to marry and have children, but that gave me pause."

He patted his head. "Baldness and high blood pressure run in my family. Nothing else that I know of." His mouth twisted in a contemplative look. "You've been here for a while. Were you ever going to tell me who you are?"

"Honestly, at first I was going to until I found out about you."

"Ouch. Any particular reason?"

"You only think about yourself. You didn't come to Ned's and Corey's assistance. You're against the boys ranch even though there's a lot of evidence that indicates how important it is and it was a pet project your grandmother started."

"What about all the thefts and even the barn fire?"

"There's no evidence pointing to the boys at the ranch, and in this country there needs to be evidence to accuse someone of a crime. Yes, some of them do things wrong, but what child doesn't? Have you ever tried to put yourself in their shoes? Corey is your cousin. He would have been a good one for you to take an interest in."

Fletcher flinched.

"I'm not so sure if the boys' suspected misbehavior is your problem. You've been vocal for a long time about the boys ranch, even before these recent events." Darcy pointed to the portrait of Luella Snowden Phillips. "Do you think she would agree with you about shutting down the ranch when she poured so much into it?"

He frowned. "She did and so did my father. Sometimes I think they forgot all about me while they were helping the boys." He surged to his feet and turned away. "I didn't mean to say that."

"But you did. You felt neglected while all the others got their attention. I can see how that could be hard on a child."

He whirled around. "You do? You don't think I was being selfish?"

"All kids need to be reassured they're loved. That is one of the things the ranch does for the boys."

"Once when I said something to my father for not coming to school to see me in a play, he dismissed it. He said it wasn't important. One of the children at the boys ranch was scared to go home and needed consoling. I was the lead in the freshman play and had worked hard so my dad would be proud of me. He never saw it. That was only one of many instances where I came in second in both my grandmother's and father's eyes. I never could please them." He avoided eye contact with her and stared in the empty fire grate.

She hadn't grown up feeling lacking in her parents' eyes, but she'd gotten a taste of what it meant to be rejected by one when she had tried to see her birth mother. Even with positive self-esteem, she'd begun to doubt herself and wondered what could be wrong with her.

Her throat tight, Darcy covered the distance between them and laid her hand on his shoulder. "I'm sorry. I sometimes have been so focused on a mission, I forget the ones around me." She dropped her arm to her side. "I'm going to be here for a while longer. I wish you would spend some time with me at the boys ranch. They always need tutors. Helping them to learn has been so rewarding for me. At least join my group. I usually help Corey and a couple of others after school."

He didn't say anything.

"Please. You might enjoy yourself." She hesitated, not sure if she should say any more. "I want to get to know you in the time I have left in town. Come with me this afternoon. I need to be there in fifteen minutes."

"Okay. I'll follow you to the ranch. If I decide

to leave, you won't have to bring me back here. You can stay."

She smiled. "Thanks, but I hope you don't leave."

On the drive to the boys ranch, Darcy kept looking at the rearview mirror to see if Fletcher was still behind her. There were boys at the ranch who had gone through what he had growing up. Corey, for one. His father didn't have time for him and the child felt neglected. She prayed that Fletcher saw some of himself in the kids and that would change how he looked at the ranch.

She parked at the house, but as she climbed from her car, Nick strode toward her, a frown on his face. Was he mad because she hadn't returned his call while she was with Fletcher today? She'd intended to later, after she saw Fletcher and told Corey about her plans. Nick hadn't returned hers yesterday, so he had no right to be upset about that.

Nick stopped a few feet from her, his glare fixed on Fletcher. "What's he doing here?"

"Visiting the ranch with me."

As Fletcher paused on the steps to the porch and waited for her, Nick focused on her. Intense. Troubled. "We need to talk."

Chapter Thirteen

After Nick informed her about the Lone Star Cowboy League's emergency meeting, he asked, "What is Fletcher doing here? Hasn't he done enough damage, trying to rally people behind his cause to shut down this ranch? Is he here looking for more to complain about concerning the boys ranch?"

"We had a nice talk today, and I persuaded him to come and see the good this place does for the boys."

"And you think he's going to change? People, especially those like him, don't." Once he'd believed what she did, but he'd been disappointed too many times to feel that way now.

"People like him?" Although she could see why Nick had said that, she became defensive.

"Set in his ways. Too proud to admit he made a mistake."

"I'm not so sure he's the only one around here like that."

"What's that supposed to mean?"

"Maybe you should..." She shook her head. "Never mind. I'm late and Corey gets anxious when I am."

He clasped her arm. "Have you told him you're seeking guardianship of him? That you want to adopt him?"

"After I tutor the boys, I will."

"And he's—" Nick glanced at Fletcher "—going to be with you?"

"No."

She spun around, marched to Fletcher and then stomped up the stairs.

"Are you dating him? I see you with him a lot." A hint of hostility echoed through Fletcher's words.

She ground her teeth and entered the main house. "He's a friend. That is all. We have a common interest in Corey." Now if only she could convince her heart that was all. "We meet in the living room."

She found Corey, Aiden and Liam Ritter, another child close to her cousin's age, sitting around the coffee table. "I brought a visitor to help me today."

Corey straightened, his shoulders thrust back. "Why?"

"Because the more help you have, the faster you'll get your homework done and then y'all can go out and do your afternoon chores at the barn. Isn't today when you take care of the goats?"

All three boys nodded.

"Then let's get busy." She gestured to Fletcher to take a place next to Corey.

Darcy helped Aiden and Corey while Fletcher attempted to explain subtraction to Liam in a creative way having to do with horses. He even drew an illustration of what he was trying to get across to Liam.

"If there are only two horses, how can you take four of them away? The rancher has to get more from the pasture with fifty. He borrows ten and adds it to his two. How many does that make now?"

Liam scrunched his forehead and squinted at the paper. "Twelve."

Fletcher grinned. "Right."

"Now you can take four horses away from twelve."

Liam quickly wrote an eight on the paper.

Corey yanked on Darcy's arm and then bent close and whispered, "What's he doing?"

"He's helping. It must be working because Liam is getting the right answers. I told Fletcher how much Liam loved horses."

"So do I. I want to learn to do tricks when I ride like you do."

"Maybe one day. First you need to become an accomplished rider."

"Nick is helping me." Corey aimed a sideways glance at her as he wrote his story about the rodeo. "Nick is a good guy. Dontcha think?"

"Sure. He does a lot for the boys ranch."

"I want to learn to be a farrier. I've been watching him take care of the horses' hooves."

"Just like us with our feet, we have to take good care of theirs."

"Yeah, we couldn't ride them otherwise." Corey bent over the paper and started to write his next word. He stopped. "How do you spell *barrel*?"

"What do you think it starts with?" Darcy said *barrel* slowly, emphasizing each letter.

"A *b*. I hear an *r* and an *l* at the end."

"Good. It's *b-a-r-r-e-l*."

The rest of the tutoring session sped by, which surprised Darcy. She didn't think Fletcher would like doing something like homework with the boys, but the more he worked with Corey and Liam, the more relaxed he seemed, and he even smiled several more times.

"Liam and Aiden, I need to talk with Corey before he helps with the goats. Will y'all show Mr. Phillips where they are?"

Fletcher went without protest, but he paused at the entrance into the living room. "You'll be joining us? I won't be able to stay much longer."

"Yes, but if you need to leave before we come, the boys are fine. Cleaning their pen and giving the goats feed are part of their chores."

When the others left, Corey asked, "Why am I staying back? Did I do something wrong?"

"Because I have something to tell you that makes me so happy and excited."

His eyebrows rose. "What? Are you gonna move here?"

"No, but the reason I came to Haven in the first place was to find members of my family. You are one of those."

"I am? How?"

"Mr. Phillips is my father. He didn't know until I told him this weekend. Some great parents adopted me when I was a baby. He never knew he had a daughter before I came."

"Then why aren't you staying here with him?"

"I have two parents in Mobile, whom I love very much. My job is there. I love helping people with their legal problems. Mobile is my home. I don't live far from a beach. My father has a boat, and he goes out fishing in the Gulf all the time."

"I love to fish. My dad...used to take me several years ago until—"

Darcy held his hand. "I love to fish too. We'll

have to go sometime." The emotions she was trying to keep in check swelled in her throat. She swallowed hard and continued, "Do you know what that makes us? We're cousins. I'm so happy we are. Being a relative makes it easier for me to apply to be your guardian."

"Guardian? Is that like a parent?"

"Yes. In fact, I want to adopt you. It takes a little longer, but I want us to be a family. You are special to me." She hugged him and then looked into his face, praying he felt the same way.

He grinned from ear to ear. "I love you."

"Back at you."

He threw his arms around her and plastered his body against her. "I'm gonna have a home?"

"Yes." Her eyes misted with tears. *Thank You, Lord, for making this easy on Corey.* When she thought she could talk without choking on her happiness, she said, "We'd better go check on Aiden, Liam and Mr. Phillips."

Corey jumped to his feet, excitement brightening his features. "Wait till I tell them I'm gonna have a home." He raced from the room. The sound of the front door opening was followed by "C'mon, Darcy."

"Coming." She swiped away the tears on her eyelashes.

As she strolled to the goats' pen, Corey ran ahead. When she arrived, the boys were inside, including Corey and Fletcher. Liam was telling Fletcher the names of each of the goats. Nick stood off to the side, leaning against the four-foot fence, his arms crossed over his chest, watching everything Fletcher did.

She came up behind Nick on the other side of the enclosure and whispered, "Has Fletcher sabotaged anything yet?"

"It hasn't been ruled out that he wasn't behind the barn fire."

"Darcy is going to adopt you?" Aiden exclaimed from the goat's pen. "When will you be leaving?"

Corey cocked his head to the side. "I don't know." He whirled toward her and Nick. "When?"

Darcy smiled. "As soon as the paperwork with the state is completed and approved."

Corey turned back to his friends. "I'll still be able to come see you."

Nick glanced at her. "He doesn't know you'll be returning to Mobile for good."

"I thought he did. I told him about my home. I'll talk to him alone later."

"I've found with kids that you have to give them exact, concrete information or directions. Don't forget the meeting. It starts in half an hour." Nick pushed off the fence, tipped his hat at her and ambled to the gate.

As he walked away, she felt as if he was walking out of her life. And she guessed he would be soon when she left for home with Corey.

Nick sat in Gabe's crowded living room as the last two people arrived—Darcy and Fletcher. With Avery's companion here, this meeting might be long and hostile.

Gabe stood, and slowly the chatter among the attendees ceased with everyone looking at the president of the Lone Star Cowboy League Waco Chapter. "With the rumors flying around Haven concerning the Avery Culpepper who has been here for the past several months, I felt we needed to meet and come up with a game plan. We all have seen how well the new expanded boys ranch is doing." Gabe fixed his gaze on Fletcher, but Darcy's birth father remained quiet. "We have to stop the land from going to developers."

As members nodded and verbally agreed, Nick watched Fletcher. The man leaned toward Darcy and said something. She gave him a small smile. What was going on with him? Most people didn't change and certainly not overnight.

Gabe continued, "That's why I've requested Darcy Hill and Lana Alvarez to explain about Avery Culpepper, the one who is in town right now."

Darcy and Lana rose and joined Gabe.

"I'm going to let Darcy explain what she discovered about the real Avery." Lana shifted toward Darcy.

"I'm an attorney who has worked with the foster care system and the state in Alabama, so I've learned how to dig in the right places for information. I uncovered that John Culpepper married a woman named Elizabeth. I've even tracked down Avery Culpepper's birth certificate. The fake Avery said she didn't have her original birth certificate and couldn't get one. The thing is, even adopted children in many states can get their original birth certificates, not just the one that has their adoptive parents' names on it. That's how I located my birth parents."

"So the rumor that you are Fletcher Phillips' daughter is true," Seth Jacobs, the secretary of the Lone Star Cowboy League Chapter, said.

"Yes. Fletcher is my biological father."

Whispers filled the room.

Darcy put two fingers in her mouth, and a loud whistle shrieked from her. Suddenly the room quieted. Nick grinned in spite of his mixed-up feelings for Darcy at the moment.

"I asked Avery to produce her birth certificate, and she refuses. Before that, I asked about her birth date and the name of her mother. She got both of them wrong. What she said doesn't match the real Avery, the one you need to fulfill

Cyrus Culpepper's will. She's still at the Blue Bonnet Inn, I called and invited her to come tonight." She swept her arm across her body to indicate the whole crowd. "As you can see, she didn't show up."

Gabe stepped forward. "Which means we don't have the real Avery Culpepper, and we have less than two months to find her. That leaves three people we still need to come to the seventieth anniversary of the founding of the Lone Star Cowboy League Boys Ranch."

"No, we only have two," Bea Brewster said. "At least I hope so. I just received a letter from Carolina Mason, a grandniece of Morton Mason. She is coming back to Haven soon. I think she'll help us with Morton."

Wyatt had been lounging against a wall. When Carolina Mason's name was mentioned, he stiffened. His mouth twisted into a frown, and he dropped his gaze as he apparently struggled with the announcement that Carolina Mason would be arriving in Haven soon.

"Okay, it looks like we might have a lead on Morton Mason," Gabe said. "We still have to locate the real Avery and my grandfather, and so far I haven't been able to find a trace of him. Neither has Tanner."

Fletcher came to his feet. "I have a good private investigator I use in my practice. I'll pay for him to look for both of the missing people to fulfill Cyrus's conditions."

Silence blanketed the room full of stunned faces. Nick couldn't believe what he was hearing. What was Fletcher's scheme now? "How do we know this isn't one of your tricks to ruin the boys ranch and shut it down?"

Darcy's gaze zeroed in on Nick, stabbing through him. "I've been showing Fletcher how important the ranch is for the boys. A person can change his mind."

Nick fisted his hands. *No, they can't. I tried and prayed so hard that my father would change.*

Fletcher grinned at Darcy. "Thank you for saying that. But I can understand why some people would be leery about this proposition. Nick has a good reason for saying that." Darcy's birth father scanned the room. "Personally I would feel the same way if I were in his shoes. If you want, I'll pay whoever you find to look for those two still missing. I came today to offer my support in fulfilling the will but also to tell you I think you're right in looking for the real Avery. She never told me, but I don't believe the woman staying at the Blue Bonnet Inn is Cyrus's granddaughter." Fletcher sat again, and Darcy laid her hand over his.

"Frankly, we need all the help we can get. I'll take you up on your offer, Fletcher. But—" Gabe made a visual sweep around the room "—I hope that Lana and Darcy will continue looking into the real Avery. Without these two, we could still be dealing with the fake one."

Several nodded while others said yes. Nick remained quiet. What happened to the woman he'd started caring for? Did Fletcher have her under his control now? He needed fresh air before he said more. Nick strode into the hallway and left Gabe's.

He was halfway to his truck when Darcy called out, "Wait, Nick."

He shouldn't. He should keep going to his pickup.

"Please."

He stopped and rotated toward Darcy, beautiful as ever. She saw only the good in people. He wished he could, but growing up with a monster for a father had killed that inside him.

How do I ignore what my dad did and move past it?

"I'm going to talk with Bea about taking Corey over a long weekend to Mobile to meet my parents and see my house. I want him to become familiar with my home before he moves there."

"When are you doing this?" He clenched his teeth so hard, his jaw hurt.

"Probably this Friday. I haven't made arrangements yet."

"Why are you telling me this?"

"I—I felt you should know where Corey is. I'll be back for Heath and Josie's wedding on Tuesday."

"Have you told Corey he'll be moving soon?"

"I want him to see my home and meet my parents first before I say anything else about moving."

"See you at the wedding then." He pivoted and marched toward his truck before he said something he would regret.

On Thursday, Darcy sat on her bed at the inn, talking to her mom. "Our plane lands at Mobile Regional Airport at 1:45 p.m. tomorrow. I want to show Corey where I work before we head for Gulf Shores and my house."

"Warren and I will be there to pick y'all up at the airport. No sense renting a car. We want to spend as much time with you and Corey as we can."

"See you then. Love you, Mom."

When she hung up, Darcy stood and slipped her phone into her jeans pocket. She wanted to talk to Carol before she met Fletcher at the boys ranch. She hated how she and Nick had parted the last time they saw each other, and Carol knew Nick. Maybe she could help her understand what was going on with him.

Darcy could sympathize with Wyatt. He'd loved Carolina, and she'd left him. Although Darcy would be the one leaving Haven, she'd stay if she thought she had a future with Nick. What if she did move here anyway? Would it even make a difference to him? She didn't think she could stay here permanently if there wasn't a future for them. Her heart would break every time she saw Nick.

Darcy found Carol downstairs in the kitchen. The aroma of coffee pervaded the house. "I hope I can get a cup before I leave."

"Of course. That's why I have it on." Carol took two mugs from the cabinet and poured coffee into them. "When do you have to go?"

"I'm meeting Fletcher in a half hour." Darcy sat at the kitchen table across from Carol. "Did Avery skip out on her bill after all?"

"Fletcher tracked down her whereabouts. She has left Texas and is heading for California. Maybe she'll be able to catch a rich man out there, but Haven is so much better off without her here causing trouble."

"You went to Fletcher about this?"

"No, he came to me early this morning to tell me she was gone for good. He even paid her bill."

"He did? Why?"

"He told me part of what happened was his

fault. He encouraged her to file a lawsuit to challenge Cyrus's will. How are you two getting along?"

"Okay. He has helped me the last two days at the ranch tutoring the boys and will again today. He's determined to teach Liam how to subtract."

"That's a surprise. Is there any more talk of shutting down the boys ranch?"

"Not to me, but then, he knows where I stand on it." Darcy sipped the delicious coffee. She would miss this every day.

"How's Nick doing?" Carol ducked her head while she stirred sugar into her drink.

"I don't know. I didn't see him yesterday at the ranch. I pulled up at the main house, and he hopped into his pickup and left. He's not happy with me because I'm going to Mobile this weekend and taking Corey to see where I live."

The clang of the spoon hitting the side of the cup resonated through the kitchen. "That's not the problem. It's the fact that you'll be permanently taking Corey away from Haven. The child has been a large part of his life since he left the army. Corey has been good for Nick, but he's also been good for the boy."

"Are you telling me I shouldn't leave with Corey?"

Carol shook her head. "When you started seeing Nick, I was thrilled. I was hoping you two would get together. That would be perfect for Corey. He cares about you both. The child might not say anything to you, but he isn't gonna like leaving Haven for an unknown place."

"That's why we're going to visit."

Carol lifted her mug and took a drink. "What happened to you and Nick? I saw you and him dancing Saturday night. I haven't seen him look at another woman the way he looks at you."

"I thought we were making progress, but lately he has pulled away from me."

"Because you announced you're leaving Haven when everything is settled concerning Corey. He went into defensive mode. Don't tell anyone, but Howard told me he's sure his nephew is in love with you."

"Nick said that to Howard?"

"Well, not in so many words, but if anyone knows Nick, it's his uncle. He's the one who helped Nick with his father."

"Nick doesn't want to be a father. I have to go where I'll have family support." If Nick wanted to be that support, though, she would stay. She had no doubt Nick loved and cared about Corey. But she couldn't stay without more commitment from Nick.

Darcy closed her eyes for a few seconds, picturing Nick the last time she had talked with him on Monday. There was a finality to his look as he turned to walk to his truck—as though he had shut his emotions down and closed himself off from her. "All I know about Nick's father was that he was an alcoholic. I think that's why he bonded so well with Corey. Nick would never tell me anything else, but whatever it was, it scarred him."

"He doesn't talk to anyone about it, not even Howard."

"There can never be a relationship between us without the truth. Not that he has lied to me. There's a lot I know about him from his caring nature and kind disposition, especially to the boys at the ranch. He would be a great father for Corey, even if he doesn't think so. But I can't fall in love with someone who shuts me out and doesn't want marriage and a family. Corey and I will be a package deal." What was sad was she'd already fallen in love with Nick, but she'd find a way to get over him and move on—for Corey.

"Tell him what you just said to me."

"My example of a loving couple is my parents. They share and tell each other everything. Sometimes they can complete each other's sentences. I won't settle for anything less. I'd rather be single than marry the wrong man."

"You want him to open up to you, but have you told him how you feel?"

Darcy sighed. "I'm still trying to figure that out. He confuses me. But Nick knows I want a family."

"Then pray about it. God is always there to help us when we need it." Carol patted Darcy's hand on the table. "Go home and see your parents. Let Corey have a mini vacation. He certainly deserves it after the past few months."

Darcy rose. "I have to meet Fletcher, but I appreciate your insight and kindness. I've grown to like Haven and especially the townspeople. When I leave for good, I'll miss y'all." She hugged Carol and then hurried from the kitchen before she got misty-eyed.

Ten minutes later when she arrived at the boys ranch, she saw Nick's truck still parked at the barn. She glanced at her watch and decided she had some time to talk to Nick since she didn't see Fletcher's car yet. Nick wasn't going to avoid her yet again.

Chapter Fourteen

Nick paused in the entrance to the tack room at the old barn. Flint had set up his temporary office inside. "I'm leaving."

"You're going to miss seeing the boys today. Like you have the last two days. What's going on? You usually prefer being here when they come."

Nick hated to admit that he was avoiding Darcy. When he saw her, he wished their circumstances were different. He'd known when she came to Haven that she was only here temporarily. He didn't plan to fall in love with her. If he stayed away from her, he'd get over her and move forward. At least that had been his plan. She would be leaving soon—with Corey. A stab of pain pierced his heart when he thought about not seeing them again.

He started to turn away when Flint asked, "Lady problems?"

Instead of leaving, Nick moved closer to Flint and lowered his voice. "Is it that obvious?"

"Like a neon sign in the dead of night. If Darcy hadn't helped Lana with Avery, we could have been in a world of hurt come March when the real Avery wasn't at the celebration. So what's wrong?"

"She's leaving and taking Corey with her when the paperwork for guardianship is finalized."

"And you don't want Corey or Darcy to leave Haven?"

"Neither of them," Nick finally admitted out loud.

"Have you asked her to stay?"

"Well, not in so many words. We haven't known each other long, so how can I do that?"

"You let her know what you're feeling for her. She can't read your mind."

"She's always wanted a family. Not just one child but also more. I'd be lousy father material." Lousy husband material too.

Flint's eyebrows slashed downward. "*Lousy?* Who in the world says that?"

"Me."

"Well, you're wrong. I've seen you working with the boys countless times. You're a natural and would make a great father. Why do you feel that way?"

"My father wasn't a good example. I never want a child to feel like I did." The last sentence slipped out before Nick could censor himself.

"You're not your father. For a long time I thought I wasn't a good dad because of all the problems Logan was having. Children can go through bad times. The key is to stick with them. Like the Lord. There are times we draw away from Him, but He doesn't give up on us. Our Heavenly Father is the best example of what a father is."

Nick wanted to tell Flint He was the exception. "What if God has given up? What if your prayers aren't being answered?"

"How do you know they weren't answered?"

"Because nothing changed. I prayed for one of my combat buddies to live when he was gunned down, but he didn't. He died while I was trying to save him."

"The Lord doesn't always do what you ask because He has a better solution we might not see. Death is part of our life cycle. You may walk away from Him, but He never does from you."

"Nick, are you in here?" Darcy called out.

"I have to go to the storage barn. I'll tell her you're in here," Flint said as he exited the tack room.

For a second panic raced through Nick. He wasn't prepared to talk to her. As he frantically searched for a way to escape, Darcy appeared in the doorway and blocked his only path. Her somber expression didn't bode well for this conversation. She'd called, and he hadn't called back. They seemed to be doing a lot of that lately—not returning calls.

But seeing her only confirmed what he'd already figured out. He loved her. In a short time they had been through a lot together because of Corey and the boys ranch. If he told her, would it make a difference in her leaving Haven?

"I know you've been avoiding me, but I wanted to remind you that Corey and I will be flying to Mobile tomorrow morning."

So soon? Stunned, his emotions deflated, he sank onto a small desk Flint had brought into the tack room. When he wanted time to slow down, it sped up instead.

"We'll be back Monday evening. I thought you should know the exact times."

Before he could make a comment, she spun around and hastened away.

A jolt of energy spurred him into action. He rushed after her and caught her before she left the barn. "Why are you taking Corey to live in Mobile? Everyone he knows lives around here." He repeated what he'd already told her, but he didn't know what else to say to her. "Corey is special to me..." He wouldn't be able to fulfill his promise to Doug.

She halted but didn't turn around. "I wanted Corey to meet my parents and for them to meet him. It might be weeks before everything is completed concerning the guardianship."

"Then you and Corey will leave for good?"

She glanced over her shoulder. "Yes. Is there a reason I shouldn't?"

"This is Corey's home. I won't see him anymore. I won't—"

"I have to go tutor. Good-bye."

"—see you anymore." He finally finished his sentence when Darcy was two yards away, but his whispered words didn't reach her. He repeated louder, "I won't see *you* anymore."

She slowed and then finally stopped, her body stiff.

He came up behind her and clasped her shoulder. The tension beneath his palm melted, and she rotated toward him. He searched her expression, but he couldn't read what she was feeling. She tilted her head back and stared into his eyes.

His throat closed at her probing gaze. Worse, though, was the silence that filled the air.

You let her know what you're feeling for her.

He scanned the yard. Surprisingly they were alone. "I'm falling in love with you, Darcy. I didn't want to. I know you want a family. I don't know if I can do that. I've been angry with my dad for most of my life. He threw his life away. Alcohol was more important to him than I was. He wouldn't stop. I wasn't enough for him to want to. When I went into the service and left home, I never wanted to see him again. And I didn't. He died before I came back home, and I was relieved." The one thing he'd held back even from his uncle spilled from his lips before he could stop.

She grasped his hand. "Why?"

"Because I can't forgive him for using me as a punching bag when he was drunk and upset."

She closed her eyes for a few seconds, and when she reopened them, tears glistened in them. "He abused you physically?"

"Yes, and mentally until I enlisted in the army and escaped. As I got bigger and stronger, the abuse was more verbal, but his words hurt every time he said them. I was the reason my mom wasted away, according to him. After having me, she never was the same."

"Did he abuse your mother?"

"He didn't hit her, but he belittled her all the time. It got worse over the years." He stepped closer. "Now you see why I have avoided any relationship that meant I had to commit to someone. I lived in a dysfunctional family and then went overseas to fight often unknown enemies. It's hard for me to trust anyone, especially with my feelings." Nick swept his arms out from his sides. "This was real hard. I want to forget the past, and each time I talk about it, I relive it."

"And I imagine that helping Corey has opened old wounds for you."

He nodded. "I didn't want you to leave without knowing how I feel. That's how much you mean to me."

Darcy cupped his face. "I'm so sorry. Thanks for telling me. That means a lot to me, but I have to have it all. I know how important a family can be."

"I wanted you to know why it wouldn't work for us. You have a good life in Mobile. Maybe Corey leaving here will be better for him in the long run. I know you'll have his best interests at heart. I trust you with him."

"Nick! Nick, you're here today." Corey raced in his direction with Aiden right behind him. "I've missed you the last couple of days." Corey threw his arms around Nick.

He embraced the child. How much longer would he be able to do this?

"Where did y'all come from?" Nick ruffled Corey's hair.

He twisted around and pointed at the school bus leaving. "Will you be here after I do my homework?"

Nick looked up at Darcy.

She mouthed the word *please*.

"Yeah, I'll even give you and Aiden a riding lesson if you do everything you need to with Darcy."

"Yay. C'mon, Aiden. Let's get our snack and do our homework."

Corey and his friend rushed toward the back of the main house.

"That's my cue to get busy. I'm glad you're going to see them later." She clasped his arm. "Go talk to Pastor Andrew. You need to deal with your anger at your father. You'll never be free if you let him control you even now. You aren't him, but I think there's a part of you that fears you are."

"C'mon, Darcy. We want to ride," Corey yelled from the back stoop, Fletcher next to the boys.

"Duty calls."

"Will you be coming down with them?"

"No, I've got to pack for the trip tomorrow morning. Y'all have guy time." She strolled away.

He watched her go into the main house. *Don't let her get away.*

He didn't move. He didn't know what to do anymore. Normally he was very decisive, but Darcy tilted his world upside down. And she was right. He had unfinished business with the Lord. When he left the ranch, he would pay Pastor Andrew a visit.

When Darcy stepped out onto her parents' back deck overlooking the water, she breathed in a deep lungful of the sea air. She loved the smell she associated with so many wonderful memories. Standing at the railing, she spied her dad and Corey on the beach walking. The past two days had been great. As she knew they would, her parents made Corey feel like he was part of the family. Corey was already calling them Papa Warren and Grandma Betty, and they loved it.

This would be a good place for Corey to grow up, and yet every time she thought that, Nick filled her thoughts, especially images of him Thursday night teaching Corey and Aiden how to ride when she snuck down to the corral for a few minutes before leaving. If only he saw what she did. He would be a terrific father, and Corey adored him—all the boys respected him and listened to him.

From the moment she had decided to adopt Corey, she'd thought of him living here where she'd grown up, in the place she had loved all her life. But then Nick had finally opened his heart to her—the one thing that had been holding her back. When he told her about his father, her heart tore as though she'd gone through the horror with him.

Thank You, God. You blessed me with wonderful parents. All children should have that. What do I do about Nick? I love him, but I love my parents and my home too. I can't live in Haven without a commitment from Nick. What is best for Corey? For me? For Nick?

Her parents were expecting her to come home. They were looking forward to being part of hers and Corey's lives. Nick didn't think he deserved that happily-ever-after.

The soft breeze off the water played with her hair as she watched Corey take off his shoes and run in the shallow water, laughing. A long sigh escaped from her.

"Honey, where are your dad and Corey?" Her mother came up behind her.

Darcy pointed in the direction of the beach. "Out there playing—again." Now her dad was shoeless and letting Corey chase him through the water.

Mom laughed. "He's having so much fun."

"Which one?"

"Both, but I was talking about your dad.

When we were going to bed last night, all he talked about was Corey."

If she stayed in Haven, it would break her parents' hearts, and would Nick ever be able to make the commitment she and Corey needed? But if she lived here with Corey, how would she ever forget Nick and move on?

"You're awfully quiet, dear. Is something wrong?" Her mother leaned against the railing while she studied Darcy, as she did when she knew something wasn't right. "Something is troubling you," she added when Darcy didn't reply.

"Mom, I'm torn between two places—here and Haven."

"You are? Why? You've only been there a short time. Is it your birth father?"

When she'd talked about Haven in the past two days, she'd mentioned all the people she'd gotten to know, but she hadn't told them what she was feeling concerning Nick because she'd been sorting through her emotions. She thought when she came here that she might realize she didn't love him. But that didn't happen. He might as well be with her. She couldn't shake him from her mind. Would distance help her with that?

"No. Remember I told you about Nick, especially his relationship with Corey? Nick and I grew very close too. I love him."

Her mother's eyes grew round. "You haven't known him long."

"Sometimes, like you and Dad, you know it in here." She patted her chest over her heart. "You and Dad were only together a couple of months before you married, and look at how long and great your marriage has been."

"We've had our ups and downs. All marriages do, but we've always been able to work our problems out. Do you feel you could do that with this Nick?"

"Yes."

"What do you want to do? Would he move here?"

"His home and ranch are in Haven. For that matter, Corey has lived in that area all his life."

"So you would stay there?"

"Yes" came out of Darcy's mouth instantly before she really considered it, and the answer felt so right. She would fight for Nick—make him see what everyone else did. He was nothing like the father he'd described to her.

"Then expect us to visit a lot."

"And I'll come home a lot, especially in the summer. Corey would live on the beach if I let him." When he had seen the water for the first time, he pumped his arm in the air and grinned from ear to ear.

"What about your work?"

"I'll find something similar in Haven or Waco after I qualify to practice law in Texas. There's the boys ranch, and if they ever start a girls ranch, I'll be involved in it too. I started riding horses again and realize how much I've missed it the past few years."

Her mother hugged her. "I'm thrilled you're riding again. You were so happy when you were doing it. When Beauty died, I was worried about you. You took it hard."

"I shouldn't have pushed her that day."

"She loved jumping as much as you did, and she was quite an entertainer."

"Will you and Dad be okay with me staying in Haven?"

"We've been blessed to have you for twenty-seven years. We knew there would come a time when you'd begin your own family. And with your dad semiretiring this year, we'll have more freedom to go where we want."

When she looked into her mother's eyes, peace settled over Darcy. She was doing what she was supposed to do. She knew that now.

Darcy sat next to Corey at the wedding ceremony for Josie and Heath at the Haven Community Church. Josie's ivory-colored gown fell in soft folds to the floor while Heath had donned his Texas Rangers' dress uniform.

The couple stood holding hands before Pastor Andrew as they exchanged their own marriage vows. Flint, the best man, gave Josie's wedding band to Heath, and he slipped it onto her left hand. She smiled with tears running down her face.

When Pastor Andrew said, "You may kiss the bride," Heath leaned toward Josie and kissed her. Suddenly he stepped back, his eyes round.

Josie laughed, taking Heath's hand and laying it on her round belly. "The baby is welcoming you to the family."

The audience, full of family, friends and Texas Rangers, broke out into cheers while Heath turned to the guests with his and Josie's linked hands raised. His face radiated a smile.

"Mr. and Mrs. Heath Grayson," Pastor Andrew announced.

When the couple began their walk down the center aisle, Corey bent close to Darcy. "Why's Josie crying?"

"Those are happy tears." Darcy turned as the newly wedded pair strolled past her.

Several pews back she caught sight of Nick and Howard, cheering and clapping. Suddenly Nick stopped, and his gaze zeroed in on Darcy. Chills streaked down her body. She hadn't seen him since before she left for Mobile. She'd been at the boys ranch all day helping with the setup for the reception. She'd hoped Nick would be there and they could talk, but through the grapevine, she'd discovered he was searching for several cows that were missing from his herd.

The audience filed out of the pews. Carol and Clarence left first, followed by her and Corey.

Walking out of the sanctuary, Carol whispered, "Did you ever talk to Nick?"

"Not yet."

Carol nodded toward where Nick still sat and whispered, "I'll make sure Corey gets to the ranch. You'll never enjoy the reception until you settle things with Nick."

Howard rose and headed to the exit while Nick stayed, his head bowed. His uncle slowed, clasped Darcy's hand and gently squeezed, then continued into the foyer.

As the wedding guest emptied the sanctuary, Darcy sat in the last row of pews. He'd stayed for a reason. She wanted to give him the time he needed. Her heartbeat picked up speed while observing him. Their last conversation hadn't settled anything. He said he loved her and trusted her judgment concerning Corey. He understood why she wanted to live in Mobile and gave his blessing. Did that mean he didn't love her enough to put his past behind him?

She wanted more. She wanted him.

* * *

The silence in the church soothed Nick for the first time in a long while. After talking with Pastor Andrew the other day, he knew he would never heal until he let go of the past and forgave his father. He'd ruled Nick's life long enough.

Closing his eyes, he instantly pictured Darcy and Corey as they sat waiting for the wedding. He'd been tempted to sit in the same pew, but he and his uncle had come in late. They'd grabbed what seats they could near the back.

He'd missed her so much while she'd been in Mobile. She was all he thought about day and night. He'd hoped when she'd decided she should move to Alabama with Corey that everything would go back to normal. But she haunted him even more than she did when she was here in Haven.

That was when he knew he had to find a solution or go crazy.

Father, help me to forgive my dad. Help me find my way back to You. I'm tired of living alone. There has to be more to life than getting up every morning, working and then going to bed at night.

The memory of his last riding lesson with Corey invaded his mind. The boys ranch had answered a need deep inside Nick. Every day, especially since Corey had arrived, he'd looked forward to helping out there—even after a long day working on his own land. The boys' smiles were all the thanks he needed.

Was this contentment when he left the boys ranch—even when things didn't go well—what it felt like to be a father, nurturing and caring for a child?

He wanted more of that. He didn't have to follow in his dad's footsteps. Being so angry with him had taken over his life. Not anymore.

Dad, I forgive you. I hope you find peace. I'm not going to let you dictate my life anymore.

He drew in a deep, composing breath and released it slowly as he let go of the rage. While doing that, he also opened his heart to the Lord. He couldn't continue going through life alone. Tranquility cloaked him.

God was here with him. A smile grew from deep inside Nick and took over his solemn expression. Now he was ready to fight for the woman he loved.

He was starting to rise when he glimpsed Darcy standing at the end of the pew. Warmth emanated from her. Words fled his mind as she came near him and sat beside him. Emotions he'd never thought he would experience crammed his throat.

"I missed you," she said in a soft voice that flowed over him.

He swallowed several times. "I missed you too." When he bent toward her, he grazed her lips with his. "You were gone way too long." He wanted to ask her about the trip but was afraid of what she would tell him.

She raised her hand and ran her fingertips across his mouth. "Well, I'm going to be here for quite a while now."

"What does that mean?" he asked, his heartbeat thundering in his ears.

"It means I'm staying here, unless you don't want me to."

He cradled her face and drank in her beautiful features while he murmured, "Are you sure?"

"I love you, Nick McGarrett. I'm very sure."

"Good, because I was contemplating moving to Alabama."

"You were?"

"I love you too. I realized I didn't want to live without you in my life. I took your advice and talked with Pastor Andrew. I forgave my father. He doesn't have a hold over me anymore. I choose not to dwell on the past and what he did." And he would fight to keep it that way.

Her smile grew. "Good. Now you can really live." She wound her arms around him and kissed him.

He poured all his feelings into it. He didn't want her to doubt his love for her.

When they parted, he laid his forehead against hers, his hands on her shoulders. "Where's Corey?"

"Carol took him to the ranch for the wedding reception. She was playing matchmaker, and I doubt Corey minded. In Mobile he told my parents all about you and how you were teaching him to ride horses. He loves you like a father."

"Is that why you're staying?"

"I'm staying because it's the best move for him but also for me. I can practice law anywhere. The ranch that you've poured money and a lot of time into is here. It will be a great place to raise Corey and call home."

"Does that mean you'd marry me?"

"Yes. When I think about that, it feels right."

"Then we won't have a long engagement."

"I agree. The whole time I was at home I thought about you. Absence does make the heart grow fonder."

He weaved his fingers through hers. "I never thought I wanted a family—a wife and kids—but now I know I do if it's with you. We both have a lot to give Corey, but I hope also other children."

Tears sparkled in her eyes. "I do too."

"Let's go celebrate. What's a better way to do that than with our friends?"

"And family. Will you be all right with Fletcher being in my life?"

"I'll make it work. While you were gone, he was at the boys ranch volunteering in your place. There's hope for Fletcher." And for the first time in a long while, he felt there was hope for him.

They rose together and left the church, hand in hand.

The minute Darcy entered the wedding reception at the boys ranch with Nick, Corey made a beeline for them.

"Where have you been? I thought something happened." Worry knit the boy's forehead.

"We had a few things we needed to talk about." Darcy felt Carol's gaze boring into her. She didn't want to say much at Heath and Josie's party, but she would have to tell Carol something.

Corey shifted his attention back and forth between her and Nick. "Is something wrong?"

Nick laughed and tousled his hair. "You worry too much. Nothing is wrong. In fact, everything is right."

"I told Nick that you and I are going to live here in Haven."

"Really?" Corey said so loud everyone around them stopped talking and stared at them.

Darcy pulled him away from the people

nearby. "Shh. Yes, but don't say anything yet. This is a reception to celebrate Heath and Josie getting married."

Nick slung his arm around Darcy's shoulders. "But we might be the next couple to marry in Haven."

Corey's eyebrows shot up. "Yes!" He pumped his arm in the air and then turned to leave. "Wait till—"

"No." Nick pinned him with a sharp look. "I'm counting on you to keep quiet until tomorrow. Okay?"

Corey nodded. "Yes, sir."

Darcy chuckled as the ten-year-old disappeared in the crowd. "I won't be surprised if the whole town knows by the time the party is over."

Nick moved in front of Darcy, blocking her view of the reception. "With Uncle Howard, Carol and Corey, I give it half an hour. I'm so happy I'm not sure *I* can keep quiet."

"Same here." All her feelings for Nick were screaming to let the world know.

Nick stared at her mouth. "I want to kiss you. Let's get some fresh air."

"We just got here," she said with a grin as she headed for the front door.

The second Nick stepped onto the porch and closed the front door, he tugged Darcy into his embrace. "I love you. I know life with you will never be dull."

She laughed. She rose onto her tiptoes and hooked her arms around his neck. The light touch of her lips whispered against his. "I love you, Nick McGarrett, and can't wait to be a family with you."

Nick pulled her even closer and kissed her with all the emotions he'd suppressed for years.

* * * * *

And don't miss a single story in the
LONE STAR COWBOY LEAGUE:
BOYS RANCH *miniseries:*

Book #1: THE RANCHER'S TEXAS MATCH
by Brenda Minton
Book #2: THE RANGER'S TEXAS PROPOSAL
by Jessica Keller
Book #3: THE NANNY'S TEXAS CHRISTMAS
by Lee Tobin McClain
Book #4: THE COWBOY'S TEXAS FAMILY
by Margaret Daley
Book #5: THE DOCTOR'S TEXAS BABY
by Deb Kastner
Book #6: THE RANCHER'S TEXAS TWINS
by Allie Pleiter

Dear Readers,

I wanted to thank the authors I had the pleasure of working with on this second Lone Star Cowboy League continuity as well as Shana Asaro, our editor on this project. I worked on the first one and had as much fun with this one as I did with that first LSCL series.

I'm a retired teacher, and I loved working and helping children. That's what this series is about. There are some kids who need extra love and attention because of what they are dealing with. Corey was one of those and got the help he needed. Nick was also a troubled child while growing up, but he wasn't fortunate enough to receive the support he needed and his past affected his present. He learned he couldn't run from it. Forgetting the past wasn't easy until he dealt with his emotions concerning it. He used what he'd learned growing up to help Corey and that in turn also made Nick a stronger person.

I love hearing from readers. You can contact me at *margaretdaley@gmail.com* or at P. O. Box 2074, Tulsa, OK 74101. You can also learn more about my books at *http://www.margaretdaley.com*. I have a newsletter that you can sign up for on my website.

Take care,
Margaret